MURDER IN THE AISLE

KRISTIE KLEWES

MURDER IN THE AISLE

Merry Summerfield Cozy Mystery, Book 1

Kristie Klewes

Hi – I'm freelance editor Merry Summerfield, and it's another fantastic day in drowsy Drizzle Bay. That's until Vicar Paul and I find Isobel Crombie lying dead in a sea of flowers in the aisle of Saint Agatha's church. Who'd kill a harmless old girl like her?

In no time flat I've scored a house-and-pet-sitting gig – Isobel's remote seaside cottage and her two darling dogs. Then I find a secret office stuffed with alarming files about car thefts and Black Ops assassins. Maybe Isobel wasn't as harmless as we all thought?

Sleuthing's more fun than I've had in ages, but how safe am I on my own now things are unraveling? Little white Bichons are hopeless attack dogs.

For more information about me and my books, go to kristieklewes.com
As always, love and thanks to Philip for unfailing encouragement and computer un-snarling, and special thanks to my friends Diana Fraser and Shirley Megget who persuaded me to try writing something different.

1

FINDING ISOBEL

N ICE LEGS!

I tilted my head to one side, and my curtain of hair flipped over my eyes in the salty spring breeze.

Nice *male* legs, I'd better add. In fact they were nice enough to admire for a few minutes longer while I considered if there was anything else I should add to the little card I'd written up for the community noticeboard.

I tucked my hair back under the brim of my sunhat and gazed across the main street that runs through Drizzle Bay on the coast of New Zealand's North Island. The southern part of the North Island, to be precise, although that might sound confusing if you're not from here.

A big waft of Iona Coppington's scrumptious baking drifted across from the café. That woman can really cook, as my hips all too cleverly demonstrate. Lemon and...coconut? Maybe. My nose was probably whiffling like a rabbit's.

I suppose I should tell you I'm Merry Summerfield – 44, freelance editor, divorced, no children – and I need more excitement in my life.

The cake aroma drifted away and the salt of the sea took over again so I crossed the first half of the street to the central barrier and got back to those legs. Yes, now I was closer they were very nice legs indeed. They started with big feet in brown sports sandals, and above them narrow ankles led up to long, strong, curving calves and the start of thighs that looked capable of supporting quite a lot of weight. Unfortunately the flexing tanned thighs were mostly concealed by a pair of khaki shorts, but that didn't stop me imagining the muscles that undoubtedly existed higher up. I mentally turned the man around and pictured a woman's arms clasped over the broad shoulders that stretched his black T-shirt to the max.

A woman who looked a lot like me. Blonde, blue-eyed, and a bit too curvy.

It's far too long since I've wrapped my arms around any man's neck.

I did say divorced, didn't I? From serial philandering, butter-wouldn't-melt-in-his-mouth Duncan Skeene. Geez, the lies that man told me! How was I so easily taken in? It knocks your confidence, something like that.

At least I've got rid of the nasty name of Skeene which I hated, and reverted to Summerfield which I always thought sounded pleasantly optimistic.

I clenched my teeth and I possibly scowled. I'm doing *fine* without a man. If I tell myself that often enough it might even start to feel true.

So I continued to stare, being somewhat starved of male company, compliments, candle-lit dinners and enthusiastic rolls in the hay.

Or rolls anywhere, really. How long had it been? At least four months since that all-too-brief encounter with Jerry Palmer that I hadn't been keen to repeat.

But the man over the road? Great legs, nice bod, and strong arms shining in the late spring sun as he did something to the top of the wrought-iron fence bordering St Agatha's Church. Probably slightly sweaty. Yum. Dark hair just visible below the back of a wide-brimmed straw hat trimmed with a rosette of red feathers.

I drew a very deep breath and tried to divert my concentration back to the ad I'd been planning. Iona's baking smelled so good I might have to buy something on my way back. Maybe a chocolate caramel square?

Digging into my bag, I pulled out the card. So far it read: 'Responsible person will mind your home and pets while you're away. Impeccable references. Extremely reasonable rates.'

Would I need to say any more? Well, a phone number of course. I wouldn't add my name in case it led to all sorts of queries and conversations with my nosy friends. Maybe just my first name, although here in Drizzle Bay I'm the only Merry I know of so even that would be a giveaway. Sinking my teeth into my bottom lip and resting the card beside me on the railing, I added 'Mary' and the phone number onto the end. Close enough, and might assure me of anonymity – for a while, anyway.

I found my eyes had gone back to watching the man attending to the top of the fence. Right at that moment he turned to one side, set down a small can of paint and a brush, pulled off his hat, and ran his fingers to and fro through his hair as though the hat was too hot.

That drew a long, low, frustrated groan from deep in my throat. It was the vicar – totally unrecognizable in his casual clothes. I was lusting after the *vicar?* Things were worse than I'd thought. Vicars are not the first men to spring to my mind when considering a good bit of naughtiness.

I clutched the card. I really did need to shake life up a bit. The sooner I found a house and some pets to look after, the sooner I could have a few days of freedom and privacy away from the watchful eyes and quelling company of my much older brother, Graham.

Don't get me wrong – it's wonderful sharing the big old family home with him rent-free after the untimely death of our parents, but Graham's life is mostly focused on his work as a lawyer. Outside that, his idea of a good time is to check over his stamp collection, and he doesn't seem willing to invite friends – male or female – home. I want some music and laughter and some distractions from my currently very staid life. It's not happening with Graham always present and I can see it's not going to.

Honestly, you should hear the long-suffering sighs if I suggest something like inviting a few people to dinner.

So I came up with this cunning plan to live on my own for a while. Days or weeks, I'm not fussy how long people need me for, but it'll give me privacy for a little misbehavior if I'm so lucky and enough money for petrol and the occasional bar of chocolate, or macadamia square, or slice of pecan pie – always supposing they're looking even more tempting than the fig and fudge cupcakes in Iona's shining glass display case.

I tore my gaze away from the vicar's legs as he picked up the paint again and resumed tickling along the top of the fence. After running over the wording on my card one final time I crossed the road to the noticeboard next to the church.

"Morning, Vicar!" I chirped as I passed close by.

I wasn't perving at your legs in the least.

It must have been acrylic paint because I couldn't smell it. He, on the other hand, smelled delicious. Even better than those cupcakes. I got a waft of hard-working man and washed cotton and that nice scent human skin gets when it's warmed by the sun. And... peppermints?

"Morning, Merry," he said around the peppermint. I heard it faintly rattling against his teeth. "Wonderful day. I always think this place is so badly named."

I provided the expected chuckle. "Well, in lovely spring weather like this, yes. But it's because of Lord Drizzle's farm which used to be the only thing around here when they came up with the name a hundred odd years ago."

The vicar had to know that. He's been at St Agatha's for about twice the time I've been notionally single. Long enough to know my name apparently – and I'm not a regular church-goer.

Hmmm. That got me wondering!

He re-settled his hat. "You'd think old Lord D would have made the most of the opportunity to claim a different name when they tracked him down and told them about the title. He could have been Lord Something-a-lot-grander. Windsor... or Buckingham..."

"Trust an Englishman to think that," I said.

The vicar is definitely English. And Jim Drizzle is such an unlikely Lord that I'm sure the 'real' ones don't know what to make of him. He's the final living member of a noble family, and as such he's qualified to take his place in the Palace of Westminster. And he does! Once or twice a year he bowls over to England, does a bit of shopping and voting, checks a few supermarkets to see if they're displaying the prime cuts of his New Zealand lamb to advantage, and then trundles home again.

"Jim Drizzle's pretty down to earth," I added, fiddling with the catch on the glass door protecting the notices pinned on the board. I removed a note about a garage sale the previous week and used the push-pins to put my own message up.

The vicar took a couple of steps in my direction, not the least bit embarrassed about being nosy as he read the notice over my shoulder. "House-minding, eh?" He offered me a peppermint from the bag he pulled from his shorts pocket as "A new career for you?"

"Hardly," I said, shaking my head to refuse the peppermint. Did he even know I was a book editor? "Just to get me away from Graham sometimes. It's not a laugh a minute living with your brother."

Then, remembering who I was talking to, I added "Not that I'm planning to misbehave," which only made it worse because it sounded as though I absolutely *was*.

And I was. If I got the opportunity, I'd be off along the new expressway to the bar in Burkeville for the evening, leaving cats and dogs (and hamsters and parrots?) to fend for themselves while I sat on a tall bar stool sliding sideways glances at anyone male, halfway attractive, and hopefully single.

"Yes," I added, pushing on through what felt like a red-hot blush. "Editing's a job I can do anywhere. All I need is my laptop. No new career for me." I took another pleasurable sniff of him. "Cattery charges and kennel fees can really add up so I thought I'd offer to look after the pets for less, provided the owners supply the food."

The vicar nodded along with my brilliant business plan, stuffed the crackling bag of peppermints back in his pocket, and rescued his brush from its precarious one-handed grip with the can of paint.

Neatly trimmed nails. No big tufts of black hair on his fingers. Nice.

I cleared my throat. "So they'll know Fido or Furball will

get the food they're used to, and that someone will be right there to take them walking, or to the vet should they need it. And I'll water the pot-plants and the garden. Collect the mail... happy to do whatever."

I glanced up at his hat-band, and now I was closer I could see it wasn't a rosette of red feathers at all. It was a fresh carnation. "I like your hat trim," I said. "But it won't last long in this sun."

The vicar (I really must stop calling him that – his name is Paul McCreagh) pulled his hat off again and glanced at the carnation.

"From Isobel Crombie," he said. "She's by far the keenest on the church flower roster. She came by earlier to freshen things up. Although..." His dark eyebrows drew together.

"What?" I asked.

'Don't say 'what?' darling, it's rude,' my dear, dead mother insisted from somewhere between my ears.

The corners of Paul's mouth pulled down. "Isobel's been in there quite a long time. I'm sure she'd have stopped by for a few words on the way out."

He deserted his job of dabbing at the arrowheads on the fence top and set down his small pot of black paint and brush in a patch of shade. It seemed to be an invitation, so together we walked up the four wide steps into the church porch and he courteously stood aside so I could enter first, although on reflection I'll bet he wished he hadn't.

I gave a strangled gasp. "Oh my God!" I blurted. Pretty bad of me in a church, but Isobel Crombie lay sprawled on the somewhat threadbare carpet runner. Her eyes stared up to heaven and all around her were shards of pottery, stems of forsythia, arum lilies, carnations, hellebores, and branches of foliage – camellia leaves, I think. The back of her head was leaking. A dark red and sticky puddle contrasted starkly with her silver hair.

Paul the vicar uttered a foul and unexpected curse, dropped to his haunches behind a pew end, and said in urgent voice, "Take cover."

I obeyed, suddenly frightened the assailant might still be around.

Paul peered in every direction, head tilted, neck tendons stretched. No sounds, no moving shadows. Only the faint swish of waves, and distant traffic. Once he was sure we were alone he looked toward the ceiling and muttered, "Never again; you promised I was done with things like this." Then he rose and walked forward to feel for Isobel's pulse.

I tried not to gag. Thank heavens he was there because I'd be screaming uselessly if I was on my own.

"Call an ambulance, Merry. And the Police," he ordered.

I'd slumped down onto one of the other pews, knees gone to jelly. Clutching my throat with one hand, I dug in my bag for the phone with the other. It skidded out of my grip and fell onto the floor with a clatter. Praying it would still work, I finally managed to tap in the emergency number and was asked which service I required. When I said Police *and* ambulance, the operator asked which I needed first.

"Ambulance?" I hazarded, my mind refusing to form

coherent thoughts. "We ... we... think she's dead, so I guess the Police need to get onto it as soon as possible, too. Or not. I don't know." I cringed. She must think I'm an idiot.

Paul was now crouched beside Isobel as though still taking cover from whoever the enemy might be.

I was quickly transferred to the ambulance and Police communications centers. It was all info and details for the next couple of minutes.

"I'll just check the rest of my church," Paul said when I lowered my phone for a few seconds. "Will you be okay? I'll only be a minute, but I might find something – or something insecure."

He rose slowly, still peering all around, and then strode off down the aisle looking incongruous in his shorts and T-shirt. He tossed his hat sideways as he walked, and it landed on one of the pews. True to his word he was back in a flash and shaking his head.

I relaxed slightly. No intruder still lurking. Good.

"She's in the Lord's hands now," he said, glancing at Isobel and then at me with grief-filled eyes. I watched as he sank to his knees, clasped his hands together, and began to ask his heavenly boss to look after her soul. Or something like that anyway. His lips moved but he prayed silently.

Once he'd finished his prayer he bent right over. This, of course, pulled the khaki shorts further up his strong thighs and tightly around his lovely taut bottom. I shouldn't have noticed, but the sight seemed to give my scattered thoughts a very welcome focus.

"I'm sorry you had to see her like this," he said, looking across at me.

I pulled my gaze away from his rear end.

"You're still okay?" he asked.

I nodded, too overcome to speak.

"It's an odd injury. Leaking only very slowly."

I looked doubtfully at the dark red puddle, holding my breakfast down by sheer force of will. I wouldn't know how fast anyone's head was supposed to leak. It looked terrible to me.

"Do you have a mirror?" he asked.

I rummaged in my over-full bag, not liking the thought that he'd poke it under her head for a better look. I passed it across but to my relief he held it close to her nose and mouth to check if she was breathing.

"If she'd been shot I'm sure I'd have heard it," he said. "And there'd be more blood, and – er – brain matter."

"Do you know a lot about gunshot wounds?" I asked, still trying not to gag. It was hard to imagine our mild-mannered English vicar stomping about the steep green New Zealand hills, shooting wild pigs or deer in his time off and then dragging them down through the trees after roping them to his back. Although maybe that's what had toned up those excellent legs?

"Chaplain in Afghanistan," he said, totally surprising me. "Not so long ago. You learn things you feel you never need to know. And never want to see again."

His taking cover by the pew suddenly made horrible sense.

"I didn't know that about you!" I said, both shocked and intrigued. "In fact I don't know much about you at all." It was on the tip of my tongue to ask more but it definitely wasn't the right time..

He closed his eyes. Then, maybe worried he'd been rude to me he opened them again and added, "Afghanistan's not something I want to stir up too many memories about."

I nodded soberly but my brain was going wild with shock. Did chaplains in the desert have to wear uniforms? I supposed they did. Black would be too hot, and far too visible to enemy snipers, not to mention they'd look like Islamic State converts.

It was no chore to imagine those long legs in dusty-colored camo trousers, tucked into the boots they always wore in army movies, and a helmet with twigs on it to disguise his outline. Where would he get twigs? And maybe chaplains didn't wear helmets anyway? Although they'd need to wear *something*. I hadn't edited any military novels for ages so my intel was somewhat lacking.

I wriggled on the thin pew cushion. I was trying not to look at Isobel's staring eyes, and kept my phone to my ear as instructed. Then the Police operator said it would be between five and ten minutes until they arrived from Burkeville.

"That's okay, the vicar's here with me. It sounds like

you're pretty busy there." I could hear other voices and signals that might be incoming calls.

"Always busy here," she agreed. "More's the pity."

"Thanks for your help, then." I disconnected, because I knew my battery was running low. As I returned the phone to my bag, my fingers contacted the smooth little pouch holding one of those old pleated plastic rain-hats women used to carry for emergencies.

Dear Mum, you were always well prepared for anything.

She must have loaned it to me such a long time ago I'd forgotten it was even there. I slid the white rain-hat out, pulled it open, and leaned far enough to lay it over Isobel's face.

Paul sat back on his heels. "No, Merry. This is a crime scene. We can't tamper with anything."

"I'm not tampering," I protested. "I'm just hiding her poor eyes. Not touching anything at all. Anyway, they're on their way from Burkeville. Five to ten minutes she said, so they must have been parked halfway here watching the traffic or something."

He looked down at the body amongst the flowers. "What I don't get," he said, "is who on earth would want to kill Isobel. And why? She lives alone, wouldn't hurt a fly. I can't imagine her antagonizing anyone to the point of an argument, let alone this sort of attack."

"You can't hit yourself on the back of your head," I observed. Gosh I'm clever sometimes.

He bent over again, pushed the unfashionable rain-hat

aside, and looked closely at her neck. Then he checked the buttons of her pink blouse and the nylons that covered her neat little legs. "No sign anyone's grabbed her. No bruises on her throat, no buttons ripped off, no ladders in her stockings. Which is good, I suppose." He shook his head, and the shafts of sunlight through the stained glass windows danced across his cheeks and forehead in red and violet washes. "No pulse, no breath on your mirror." He handed it back to me and re-positioned the rain-hat. "Maybe we could have tried rescue breathing or CPR, but she's been in here quite a time and I've seen enough head wounds to know that wouldn't have worked."

In the dim shadowy light of St Agatha's he looked very large and strong and wasted on being a vicar. Although, no, I was thinking of Catholic priests, wasn't I... I was all of a dither and you can't blame me – not with poor Isobel lying there dead.

"This is very strange," he added. "She lives out on The Point. Cute cottage, but isolated. A much better place to murder her." Then he realized what he'd said and clapped a hand across his eyes. "Sorry, Merry. Ridiculous and awful thing to suggest."

"Shock," I murmured.

"Probably," he agreed, peering guiltily over his hand as he pulled it away. "It's still a lovely place though. Wild and untamed for the most part, although she keeps an amazing garden – a lot of which ends up here, I suspect."

We looked at each other glumly. "Thanks for making the

phone call," he added. "I lost it for a moment, for obvious reasons. Then it seemed more important I checked the rest of the church."

I thought he'd done better than me, especially once he'd mentioned Afghanistan. How brave did you have to be to cope with something like that?

THE TRAFFIC MUST HAVE BEEN light because the Police arrived almost sooner than they'd estimated and the ambulance wasn't too far behind.

"Next of kin?" the athletic-looking WPC asked as things swung into action and photographs were taken by a very large male constable. He'd lifted the rain-hat off Isobel's face and set it to one side. For sure I wouldn't be reclaiming it.

Paul had closed the church doors to assure privacy. "She has a sister," he said. "Margaret Alsop. Also on the church flower roster. Would you like me to...?"

"Would you?" the WPC asked. She was wearing a badge that said Moody. "It's the job I dread most, informing the families."

He produced a phone from his shorts pocket, pushed the peppermints back in when they threatened to escape, and scrolled until he found the sister's name. Of course I eavesdropped like mad because his English voice was beautiful – deep and serious and quite BBC.

"Margaret? It's Paul McCreagh from St Agatha's."

I watched as he drew a long breath and closed his eyes.

"No – nothing to do with that, I'm afraid. Look, can I pop over home and see you? It's about Isobel. I'm afraid I have some bad news."

He pressed his lips together as he listened to her reply. "Not a good idea right now, Margaret."

Then I saw him shake his head. "Okay, I'll meet you outside the church. See you soon."

"Dammit," he said, sounding very un-vicarish. "She's over at the shops and was wondering what the Police and ambulance people were doing here. I'll try and keep her away, but it won't be easy."

"And it won't make any difference," the ambulance paramedic said. "Definitely dead. No-one could have survived an injury like this. Keep her talking long enough for us to get her sister off the floor and away from that blood." He turned and spoke over his shoulder to the WPC. "Is that all right with you? You don't need her for anything else right now?"

WPC Moody lifted both thumbs, which I thought looked a little flippant considering the occasion, but she added, "We've got the photos. Be careful you don't touch anything else. I'll come with you, Vicar. We can tell her together." She looked across at me. "I'll be back to take your statement."

"Can I go as far as the door for a while?" I asked. "I could do with some fresh air and not being quite so close to her."

"Yes, no probs," she said. "There'll be more questions to follow, but that's Homicide's territory now."

Paul led the way out and she rapidly caught up with him

on her muscular legs, leaving me to tag along behind. As we reached the steps he bent and tweaked a couple of small weeds from one of the big pots sitting there.

St Agatha's has beautiful gardens around its foundations. Right now there was an edging of white primulas and behind them an absolute blaze of orange calendula. I couldn't help imagining the church was a rocket blasting off for heaven. Orange flames, white smoke. And surely Isobel's death had affected me more than I'd reckoned because that's not the way I usually think.

I stood there between the pots for a few seconds, and then, feeling pretty wobbly around the knees, sank down and sat on one of the steps and took some deep breaths of salty air. The other two went out into the sun to their horrible task. Eight or ten Drizzle Bay-ites stood clustered close by, pretending they weren't lurking or listening.

I heard the poor sister's exclamation of distress and horror all too clearly. She was a shortie like Isobel, but with silver hair in a much more expensive cut, and dressed with more style and quite a lot of jewelry. Nice jewelry. I sneaked an envious look at the bracelet she wore – one of those where you buy the basic chain and then have to spend an awful lot more on all the charms and beads to thread onto it. A total status symbol and hers showed she had plenty of status because it was stuffed with glittering bits and pieces. A couple of thousand dollars' worth at least. Maybe more. Someone loved her, or else she loved herself plenty.

Terrible way to think, Merry! She's just lost her sister. No fancy bracelet makes up for that.

Vicar Paul and WPC Moody had each taken one of her arms and were possibly trying to keep her standing up. They were certainly trying to keep her away from the church, but she was tugging at them the way the spaniels always tugged at Graham when they were out for a walk. Then I heard the paramedics quite close behind me so I pushed myself up to get out of their way.

"No, you're okay – stay," one of them said, but I got up anyway. They were wheeling Isobel on the ambulance stretcher now and had stopped not far inside the church doors, well away from the puddle of blood. Obviously they expected her sister would come into the church for some privacy and they were right. I don't know why I went back in with them; maybe I expected more questions. Paul closed the doors again.

People say strange things in stressful situations. Margaret chose to stare at her sister and wail, "Izzie, your timing is terrible. You know Tom and I are off on our cruise in a couple of days. What are we going to do now?"

Paul and WPC Moody looked at each other with raised eyebrows. "How long is the cruise?" Moody asked.

"A week," Margaret said, dabbing at her eyes with a paper tissue which she'd produced from the pocket of her expensive looking cream linen skirt. "We can't go now of course. What would people say? And there are her dogs to worry about, too."

"A week until a funeral isn't unusual," Paul said, placing a consoling arm around her shoulders as she broke into renewed sobbing. "Often there are relatives who need to travel, so then the service is delayed for a few days. It would be a shame to cancel your cruise. I know how you and Tom have been looking forward to it. It won't be quite the same of course, but you said it was the first reunion of the three brothers in more than thirty years. It would be terrible to let them down."

She sniffed and shuddered, and reached out to touch her sister. The paramedic and WPC Moody both stepped forward to prevent her, so she drew her fingers away and blew her nose on the tissue again, shaking her head.

"Can't contaminate the body," the WPC murmured apologetically.

"I'll be happy to conduct the service," Paul said. "I doubt she'll be released for burial straight away?" He looked at the WPC for guidance, and she nodded.

"Things to do yet," she said to Margaret. "If you make the funeral arrangements then we'll liaise with the vicar, and I'm sure everything can go ahead the day after you get back, if that's what you'd like."

Margaret sobbed and wailed some more.

"Can I find Tom for you?" Paul asked.

"He's at the bowling club," she said through her tears. "What a thing to happen. Poor Isobel." She dabbed her eyes again and added more calmly, "There's no point disturbing him until lunchtime."

"How about I suggest some funeral directors, then?"

She pulled herself together a little more. "Thank you Vicar, but we'll use the same people we had for Dad. They did a nice job."

WPC Moody seemed happy with that. "Be sure to say that Isobel's with – er – *us* for a little while," she said with careful diplomacy.

"I really think that's the best scheme," Paul said. "Make your arrangements, go ahead with your holiday, I'll choose a couple of her favorite hymns, and everything will have fallen into place by the time you return."

"No, that's terrible," Margaret said, starting to sob again. "What will people think?"

"That the timing is most unfortunate and you've made a sensible decision," he replied kindly but firmly.

"But the little dogs!" she wailed. "Itsy and Fluffy. They'll have to be taken to kennels somewhere. They'll never understand." She turned her face against Paul's impressive bicep.

"We might have a solution to the dog problem," he said, patting her shoulder. "Ms Summerfield here, who was with me when I discovered Isobel, takes on short-term house minding and pet feeding jobs." He sent me the slightest of winks. "Are you by any chance free for the next week, Ms Summerfield?" Then, while I was still nodding with surprise, he checked with the very large constable who'd just joined the WPC. "Would that be acceptable to the Police? I'm assuming you'll want to examine her cottage for any useful evidence."

"Aye, for sure," the constable rumbled. He sounded like

he'd been imported from Yorkshire or somewhere else in the north of England. "I don't suppose the deceased has a handbag here?"

"For house keys," WPC Moody inserted.

"In the vestry, I imagine," Paul said. "I'll get it for you. There was no sign anyone entered the church through the other door, by the way – I checked it was locked as soon as we found Isobel."

The two men walked toward the back of the church together and Margaret turned to me. "If you really could look after the dogs then I'd be very grateful. I'd pay you in advance?"

She looked so hopeful I immediately offered to do it for free – it would get me away from Graham, after all – but she turned me down, so I lowered my price a bit and said, "Ten dollars per dog, per day, plus food. And that would include walks, of course."

She nodded, and started fumbling in her handbag. "I'm sure there'll be plenty of food for them at the cottage, but if there's not..."

"I'll keep the receipts and you can reimburse me," I said as she began counting out twenties. It'd be a miracle if I ever had a hundred and forty in cash in my purse, but I guess she's a generation older than me and not so keen on paying by plastic. And, mmm... maybe no tax if this was an untraceable job for cash. Suddenly I liked the look of my new career even more, even if the cottage was 'isolated' as Paul had said. I'd be okay, wouldn't I?

2

A COTTAGE OF MY OWN

AND THAT'S why I found myself driving out to The Point late the next afternoon with a couple of changes of underwear, a nightie, and spare T-shirts. There'd be plenty of time in the days following to pop home and replenish my wardrobe once I'd settled in and decided what I really needed.

The very large constable (Henderson on his badge) had brought the keys and Isobel's two little white Bichons to me at home while anyone who needed to check out the cottage did their thing. The Bichons and the spaniels got on remarkably well together once a lot of mutual sniffing was out of the way.

I decided I had Paul to thank for quite a lot, because surely people who find bodies aren't generally given the run of the victim's property the next day? I suppose it was reasonably straightforward though. Isobel had been seen alive and presumably well – and probably by people other than Paul as she parked her elderly Mini and carried her big bunch of flowers through the village center. No doubt the Police had had a good ask around. If you can't trust a vicar's word then it's a poor outlook for the rest of the population.

PC Henderson told me the cottage had been searched and nothing was found amiss. He said it had been locked up securely, that the open windows had serviceable safety catches, there was no sign anyone had broken in, and no blood anywhere. I wasn't the least bit spooked when I drove my new aubergine Ford Focus – a somewhat guilty purchase after Graham and I had inherited our parents' savings – along the winding coast road. The little dogs seemed perfectly content in the car.

Seagulls swooped and dipped over the crashing waves visible on some of the bends. There were cliffs on my left for the first part of the journey, and bunny-tail grass and bright yellow lichen decorated the lower rocks. Then the land levelled out again and low-crouching *ngaio* bushes sprawled over some of the shingly ground; big dark green cushions impervious to the relentless salt spray. Bent and battered pohutukawa trees clung to rocky perches, a few unseasonal tufts of distinctive scarlet flowers just breaking out of their fat gray buds. In a few weeks they'd be a sea of tossing red.

I passed Sunny Cove where Graham and I had been brought to picnic as children, and then less than romantically named Drain Gully which was a well frequented 'lovers' lane' with lots of isolated parking spots. I'd only once had the dubious pleasure of being courted in Drain Gully, but you can bet if someone like me knew about it then the local Police did too and probably spoiled quite a lot of teenage fun. I was kind of tempted to turn in there and have a quick look in daylight for old times' sake, but time was getting on so I kept driving, finding the road unfamiliar now. I was a little surprised at how long it was taking to get where I was going. After many more bends I found an official road sign pointing at right angles to Drizzle Bay Road. What? Had I come the wrong way? I'd been so sure of the route I hadn't thought to check my GPS. Drawing level I found I'd been on 'Drizzle *Beach* Road'. Not helpful, people! At least I was nearly there now.

A shiny black pick-up truck crouched fifty or so yards from the cottage beside a well- weathered sign saying Beach Access. I slowed down again and gave it a suspicious glare. A path dived down between two gnarled karo trees, and there were surf-casting rods strapped to a rack on the roof of the truck. In my newly acquired role of semi detective I decided the truck looked authentic enough and perfectly safe. It had lots of chrome bars and assorted sporty logos. Expensive and well cared for, it was probably the toy of a bored, retired businessman with money to burn. A fishing rod hadn't been the murder weapon, and surely a killer wouldn't hang around the district to go fishing afterwards? I dismissed it as being of no interest.

Thirty seconds later I turned in beside the very pretty cottage. Not in the best of repair, but absolutely oozing charm; strung around with climbing roses and propped up by tall hollyhocks.

I'd never been as far as The Point. With good accessible places further back I suppose our parents had simply held all the family picnics where it was easy and safe – Sunny Cove, mostly. No boyfriend had ever driven me here for a bit of private snogging either, more's the pity. It was totally new territory, and a lot nicer than Drain Gully.

The late afternoon sun poured down, making the stems of salt-burned grass glitter like shiny wires in the sea breeze. I cut the engine, pulled on the handbrake, and slid out. Against the sun's fierce glare the air was moist and misty with sea spray. Waves pounded onto the sand at the base of an incline at the end of the property. Seagulls wheeled and screamed above me, and over the noise of the birds and the crashing water the dogs started frantically barking, knowing they were home. They jumped out of the car, raced up the path, and wriggled through the smallish pet door. Then they dashed back, telling me they couldn't find Isobel. They fell silent, heads on one side, black eyes beadily inquisitive against their snowy coats.

"I know I'm not her," I said, bending to let them sniff my fingers again. "Sorry. But at least I'll get your dinner for you."

They really were lovely little dogs. One of them sneezed, having possibly gotten too much of a whiff of my hand lotion, and the other growled a bit to show he was doing his guard duty, but they led me happily enough to the front door, bouncing along like a couple of little white teddy bears.

The bunch of keys had several possibilities. There was the obvious car key and the garage remote. PC Henderson had told me he'd driven Isobel's Mini home and garaged it so mine would have to be parked outside. There were two ordinary looking door keys, something small that might be for a suitcase, and a very old brass one that could be anything. Of course it was the second door key I needed, and the dogs encouraged me with yaps and whines and pants while I fumbled around fitting the possibilities into the lock. The dark fingerprint powder around the door handle didn't help, and there was more inside so I mentally added some cleaning to my list of duties once the Police gave me the okay. They'd taken my prints at the local Police station seeing I'd been at the murder scene, but I couldn't imagine they'd be much help. I'd never been to the cottage, and I was only rarely at Saint Agatha's.

"Hold on, hold on," I muttered, setting down my bag beside a big bucket of cold water on the white-painted kitchen table.

Hmmm, floating leaf fragments. She'd probably given the flowers an overnight drink before setting off to the church with them.

Itsy and Fluffy had name-tags hanging from their collars – gold for one dog and silver for the other – but I didn't fancy trying to read them until their tummies were full and their sharp little teeth were less likely to nip me.

"How are you doing, doggies?" I asked with no hope of an answer except encouraging barks. The silence needed filling.

Paul had been right about the location being isolated. "Are you going to be good doggies for me?"

Kill me now! What would I do if they said 'no'?

I quickly replenished their big water bowl and located a container of Pup-E-Love in the pantry. Their food bowls had been polished clean by small pink tongues so I pushed them further apart to prevent squabbling and tipped a good sprinkle of kibble into each. The little dogs fell to eating quite happily, with no idea their beloved mistress would never be returning to feed them again. Feeling horrible about that, I sneaked outside while they were occupied, wanting to check out my new surroundings before the sun got any closer to setting.

I didn't expect to be checking out the long lanky form and smooth tanned muscles of someone who looked a lot like a younger Jon Bon Jovi. With a nipple ring.

Heavens to Betsy – what a hunk!

The man paused at the top of a path that had been cut into the slope leading down from Isobel's vegetable garden to the sea. He wore almost nothing and carried a surfboard. The lowering sun lit up his flowing mane of streaky blond hair – wet in parts and curling up and floating in the late afternoon breeze in others. I stopped dead in my tracks. Who was he, and what did he think he was doing here on private property?

And could he kill me by whacking me with that surfboard?

He rested his weight back on one foot, which pulled the

muscles of his thigh into high relief. "Evening. Are you related to Miss Crombie?" His voice was deep and strong, and definitely North American.

"No. Er... just helping out."

His eyebrows drew together in a fearsome frown. "Have you bought the place?" he demanded, none too politely.

"No... I..."

"She knew I wanted it," he interrupted. "I've asked her about it every time I've seen her."

Had he indeed? How brusquely had he asked Isobel to sell? He looked pretty fierce, standing there full of belligerence and testosterone. More than a match for little Isobel. He could have snapped her neck with those two big hands. Although, I remembered sensibly, her neck hadn't been snapped at all. Someone had thumped her on the back of the head with something heavy. "Blunt force trauma," the ambulance attendant had said before backing off and adding, "but that's not my call."

"Wanted to buy it? Her house?" I asked, pushing my hair back over my shoulders. He had almost more hair than me. "I'm not surprised she didn't want to sell it to you. It's a piece of paradise."

"Which is why I want it." He glared at me with very blue eyes which were eerily illuminated by the lowering sun. He seemed not at all worried he was wearing only a pair of thin and low-slung board shorts. It was hard not to moan after my long man-drought. The wet shorts were hanging so low that the vee of abdominal muscle some men have was all on display, and very nice it was, too. My fingers itched to trace those lines down his hard flat belly, and I mentally slapped myself, moving my attention up to the taut six-pack above. Which was also very touchable. Plainly I'd been editing too many romances.

Stop it, Merry!

I swallowed. "It's not a young man's house," I said, frantic to distract myself.

An arrogant sneer stretched his lips. "You can say that again! I'd bowl it. Or do a progressive reno to make sure the original place disappeared so slowly it never became a demolition." His expression softened. "Lots of glass and timber. Some feature stone maybe. South Cal style, like me. You wouldn't get permission to rebuild here."

I could see that. It was the only house for quite some distance – idyllic but isolated. No doubt some well-meaning local authority official would consider it their duty to return the land to 'its natural condition'.

"Yes, the vicar said it was a beautiful spot."

"That hypocrite, Paul McCreagh?" The belligerence was back in full force after his wistful musings over renovations.

"What?" I demanded.

'Don't say 'what?', darling,' the dear departed Mrs Summerfield reminded me again.

But the surfer had really shocked me. "He's a vicar. And a chaplain in Afghanistan!"

"Well hallelujah. So he says. As far as I'm concerned he's just bad for business."

"Surfing business?" I asked, somewhat emboldened by Bon Jovi's obvious distaste for a very nice man.

"Liquor business. Hospitality business. Erik and I have owned the Burkeville Bar and Grill for a while now, and I'm planning on buying him out. We can do without McCreagh mooching around, nursing a soda for an hour, and turning his long nose up at anyone who's having a good time."

The penny dropped. Those startling blue eyes and tanned skin. Put him in a tight T-shirt and pull his hair back in one of those 'man-bun' things and this was the barman at the Burkeville. I'd only seen him a few times and assumed he was a tourist passing through and picking up casual work. Having placed him now I relaxed a little. And he was part owner rather than just a barman.

Okay, I'm a snob.

"Ah," I managed. Brilliant conversationalist I am when faced with an uber-handsome man. I didn't think I'd done too well with the vicar either. Out of practice – hopefully that was the answer.

I eyed the surfboard under his arm again. Could he have swung it at the back of Isobel's head to get her out of the way of his hoped-for acquisition of the cottage? How solid was a surfboard anyway? He continued to stand there as though it weighed nothing at all. From somewhere in my editing past I dredged up the information that they had polystyrene centers for flotation and that the coating on the outside was pretty thin. Which is why sharks could chomp right through them. Not that he could have carried it into the church unnoticed. I was definitely losing my marbles.

"Anyway," I said, dragging my brain back to the current situation, "Why do you say 'so he says', about the vicar? It'd be easy enough to find out whether he was in Afghanistan or not. I could Google him."

"You go right ahead and do that."

Talk about arrogant! But then his gaze dropped to my feet, slid up my ankles and calves, practically stripped my dress away when he hit thigh level, and lingered on my two best features. I had no option but to grab a fast breath, which naturally caused some inflation, and by the time he reached my face he had a devastating grin on his. What a *flirt*.

"What's your name?" he asked.

"Summerfield." I didn't think he deserved my first name after being so rude about Paul. I might have been a bit sharp with him, and I knew I wasn't too glam right now, but I was looking forward to turning up at his bar and showing him I polished up okay. "And you are...?" I asked in a voice dripping with honey. Maybe honey with a bit of arsenic stirred in.

"John," he began. It sounded more like 'Jaarn', and I promptly gave a badly-suppressed snort. Surely he wasn't going to say anything that sounded like Bon Jovi?

"Bonnington," he finished.

Close enough to make me drop my head and grin, before I raised it again and gave him what I hoped was a cool stare.

"Are you using Isobel's path as a shortcut? I saw a truck a little way along the road. Yours?"

He regarded me with those blue eyes and nodded slowly. "Yup, that's my pickup. So? It's on public land." The nipple ring winked as the setting sun caught it. "Maybe I'm just cutting through, because I've been hoping Miss Crombie might change her mind."

"Selling the house isn't in her power any longer. You do know she's dead? I'm sure you get all the gossip in the bar." I clenched my hands until my nails bit into my palms.

"Yup – main topic of conversation last night."

"So you see why I can't tell you anything. It's not my business." I edged a couple of steps away.

He took a step closer.

I'm five-eight but he was considerably more, even barefooted.

"She hasn't gone and willed it to the church or anything stupid like that, has she?"

I'm sure I gaped a few times like an out of water fish. "Why would you think that?"

"You mentioned the vicar. Smarmy McCreagh. I wouldn't put it past him to suggest it as a possibility."

"While she arranges the church flowers?" I needled, incensed on Paul's behalf. "She's not the only one who did that for him. Her sister's on the flower arrangement team, too."

"Geez, what's *she* got that he wants?"

I stared at him, thinking, '*Well, she hasn't got a sister any more*'.

Then I turned away, wanting to be done with him and deciding the rest of my property inspection could wait until the morning. I had no idea he was following me, padding along silently on his bare feet, until I heard his sharp curse.

"Dammit – has the house been broken into? Much damage?"

I whirled to face him again. "No, it hasn't, so you can stop worrying about a place you don't own and which is none of your business." But to my consternation he stepped closer, peering at the mess of fingerprint powder around the door handle.

"Are you okay, Ms Summerfield?" he asked over his broad golden shoulder. "I know what this is. When we've had trouble at the bar we've had to go through the same routine. What's been happening here?"

Then he turned around fully and I saw the genuine concern in his amazing eyes. For some reason I gave a half-hiccup, half-sob. Maybe the stress of the day was catching up with me. Talk about feeling like a nerveless Nellie...

At that moment either Itsy or Fluffy wriggled through the dog door and snagged his attention for a second or two but he turned almost instantly back to me. "You've gone pretty pale. Need something to drink and a sit-down, maybe? Come on – you do the sitting down and I'll see what's available."

"Are you always so darn bossy?" I demanded, because by

now he'd leaned the surfboard up against the house, opened the door, patted whichever dog it was, and was waiting for me to go inside.

"Probably," he agreed. "I'm used to getting things done."

I gave a bit of a sniff and then felt a tear running down my face. Of all the times to turn into a helpless female... I tried to wipe it away so he wouldn't see it but his sharp blue eyes missed nothing.

"So – tea or coffee, or something stronger?"

"Tea's fine," I croaked. "I've no idea where everything is because I've barely arrived. There might be brandy or whisky somewhere? I could look?"

He quirked an eyebrow at that and followed me in, noting the fingerprint mess on the inside of the door as well. Both dogs were now circling his feet, growling and yipping. "Oh come *on*," he said, smirking down at them. "I've got two German Shepherds who'd eat you for breakfast."

"My brother's got two spaniels," I said for no particular reason.

"Is this a dog contest?" he asked, strolling across to the kitchen counter, hefting the red enamel kettle, and filling it under the tap. It was a gas stove. I hadn't used one in ages but he seemed to know how to flick it on. He set the kettle to boil while I searched the cabinet in the dining room. It held half a dozen small fancy glasses and one partial bottle of sweet sherry. Nooooo...

I returned to the kitchen, shaking my head before sagging down onto a white-painted chair with a rather uncomfortable spindle back. Was I slightly hysterical? For some reason it was hard not to giggle at the thought of all the pairs of dogs.

"Were you planning to drown these two?" he asked, glancing from Itsy and Fluffy to the bucket of water. A grin tugged at the corners of his mouth.

I managed a shaky smile for him. "Church flowers, I think. Tip it out if you like."

It was getting darker. And here I was in a strange house with a strange man who was barely clad. Possibly not a great start to my house and pet minding career, but it was oddly good to have some company. To my surprise he didn't empty the bucket into the sink but carried it outside. I heard it sloshing in several doses onto the garden.

"She had some strawberries and blueberries coming on out there," he said when he brought it back inside. "May as well juice them up. She showed me last time I was here."

I hadn't expected that. "How long ago?"

He set the bucket in a corner. "Monday morning." And then added, "My day off."

I wiped at a couple more tears which had insisted on leaking out.

He took a pretty china teacup and a squat brown mug from one of the glass-fronted cupboards and tossed a teabag into each.

There was a roll of paper kitchen towels on the opposite counter, so I reached out and tore one off so I could blow my nose. I'm sure Drizzle Bay village would have been awash with gossip about the ambulance and Police being called to the church. I dabbed at my eyes again while he waited with surprising patience. "They're not sure quite how or why yet, but she's definitely dead. I saw her. And the Police will have fingerprinted the door here to see if anything matches with any prints on the murder weapon, I suppose."

"When did she die?"

"Yesterday morning sometime. I went into the village to put a notice on the community board. The vicar was painting the fence – all those little arrowheads on top of it. I stopped to talk for a minute and he mentioned she'd been inside for a long while, so we went into the church – partly to check she was okay, and partly to ask if she ever needed a house-and-pet sitter because he knew about the dogs. She was lying there dead with her head leaking blood."

Now it was my turn to draw a breath – a deep shuddering one – as the image of poor Isobel swam into my brain again.

"Blood? She was walking around bleeding? Didn't anyone notice?"

I shrugged at that. "I doubt she was *walking around* bleeding. It was thoroughly weird because the vicar had seen her going in, carrying a big bunch of flowers, and probably other people had seen her too. The Police would have asked around. The vicar was busy painting. She was juggling her flowers. Maybe he didn't want to hold her up if was a big armful, although she stopped long enough to give him a carnation for his hat. Perhaps she had a hat on, too?"

I hadn't thought of that before. Could it have been out in

the vestry with her handbag?

"Poor old dame," John said, pursing his lips and turning the gas down because the kettle was starting to shriek. The dogs were protesting from the pink and blue polka-dotted dog bed they'd settled into but calmed down as the noise died away. "I really liked her, but it makes it difficult trying to buy the house now. I suppose there'll be a heap of legal messing around." He looked gloomy as he poured the boiling water into the cup and the mug and pushed the cup toward me.

"Sugar? Milk?" I asked. He shook his head so I decided to go without as well. I'd turned into a total wimp but he didn't seem to mind too much. As he'd said, he was used to getting things done.

"So... how?" he asked, sitting down opposite me.

OMG – he now looked entirely naked above the table top. Delicious, but how would I stop staring?

I dabbed my eyes again to bring the view into better focus, because why waste a sight like that? "It looked like she was hit on the back of her head. The ambulance man said 'blunt force trauma', but then he backtracked because it's not his job to do the official examination and decide the cause of death."

By now I'd decided that unless John Bonnington was a very good actor it wasn't him who'd attacked Isobel. He might have been putting a bit of pressure on to try and get her to sell him the house, but he knew about the strawberries and blueberries in the garden, and had bothered to water them, and seemed genuinely saddened by the thought of her being dead.

Although what's to stop a guilty man from putting on a good act? I was trying to see things from both sides.

"I wonder who gets the place now?" he speculated. "McCreagh *might* have talked her into leaving it to the church. She had no kids. Only the one sister I think. It'll be her I suppose."

"Margaret," I said. "Margaret Alsop." I'd remembered the name from the Kirsty and Phil house-finding program on TV.

John's gaze sharpened again. "Not Tom Alsop's wife?" He took a sip of his tea and grimaced. Maybe he was a coffee man? Or hoping for whisky.

I watched as his throat constricted and his Adam's apple bounced up and down. Why do men have them and women don't? Something else I needed to Google. I prodded surreptitiously at my throat. Do women simply have fleshier necks so whatever's going on inside doesn't show?

"I think she said he was called Tom," I agreed. "He'd gone to bowls."

"Alsop A-One Autos," John said, curling his lip. "His time would have been better spent attending to business. Word gets around..."

My ears pricked up at what was possibly useful information, and I straightened up and tossed my damp paper towel into the bucket in the corner. "Why do you say that? Was the business in trouble?"

He shook his head. "Might only be rumors. Tom Alsop does himself no favors though. Made a few enemies. Always showing off in the bar. Buying people too many drinks and insisting loudly on the best brands. Good customer for us, but I don't like the guy." John sipped again. "I've heard he's real slow at paying his bills. When you're working somewhere like the Burkeville you get all the stories."

Huh – so maybe Tom Alsop also needed considering in the case of Isobel's death. I wondered how much he owed and how I could find out.

"Wears a lot of rings," John added, pressing his lips together as though ring-wearing was a crime. Plainly a nipple ring didn't count.

I thought of Margaret's bracelet. Hmmm. Flashy people needed money if they wanted to keep up appearances. Inheriting a beachfront property – even one not in top condition – would buy a lot of bling and booze.

John took another gulp of tea. "So how do you fit into the scene? I mean – what are you here to do?"

I set my teacup down with care and glanced toward the dog bed. I'd had two fingers caught through the curly china handle for a while and didn't want to tip the cup over. "Looking after these two guys," I said as I carefully extricated my fingers. "I'd gone to put a notice on the community board offering to mind houses and pets for people who were away from home."

"Pretty fast result," he muttered.

I might have gone a bit pink at that stage. "Not what I was

expecting to happen at all. One thing led to another, and then to another. We found Isobel, called the cops and the ambulance, the vicar got hold of the sister because she's on the flower roster too, and when she turned up she started going on about bad timing because she and her husband were off on a week-long cruise." I looked at him across the top of the tea-cup. I'd stupidly stuck my fingers through the handle again.

"Sounds a bit cold."

"Give her a break – she must have been in shock. She'd just lost her only sister."

"I guess... So bye-bye cruise. Bad luck Tom."

I grinned at his all too obvious satisfaction. "No – they're going. Both the vicar and the WPC said they thought they should."

John's eyebrows rose. "Sounds even colder."

"Well, poor Isobel has to be autopsied, I suppose. They can't bury her until that's done. And the vicar pointed out that funerals often don't happen until some days after the death because people had to travel to get there. So..." I shrugged.

"Which still doesn't explain how you scored the job."

I glanced toward the dog bed again. "Margaret got worked up about finding kennels to take Itsy and Fluffy while she was away, and the vicar pointed out that I could look after the house and the dogs until they got back and settled things."

"Itsy and Fluffy?" John repeated. Very softly, and trying not to grin.

"Hey – she liked things pretty," I said, waving a hand at the china cups, the hollyhocks practically climbing through the kitchen window, and the dotty dog bed. "What are yours called?"

He looked me straight in the eye. "Fire and Ice."

Yeeeesss... Masculine and to the point. Why would I have expected otherwise? "Better than my brother's dogs," I conceded. "The little girl next door named them. Daniel and Manual. To rhyme with spaniel."

The brown mug had been halfway to John's lips, but he gave such a sudden yelp of laughter that some of the tea jumped out and landed with a splash on the table-top and points south. "Manual?" he asked as I reached across and ripped another paper towel off the roll.

"Yes – she wouldn't go for Manuel. She said 'Man-well' didn't rhyme with spaniel."

John patted some spots of tea off his belly and possibly his shorts. I didn't like to peer too closely. Then he soaked up the small puddle on top of the painted timber table. His shoulders shook and his lips curved in a wicked smirk.

"He compromised on Manny and Dan," I assured him. "He pretends they're American, like you are. The dogs can tell those two names apart, and that's probably what matters most."

John glanced at his watch – a big and no doubt waterproof

stainless steel one – and then transferred his gaze to me. "Hate to say it but I'd better be going. Surf was so good I begged off bar duties for an hour or two. You okay on your own?"

I pushed the chair back so I could stand. There was a flurry of barking from the dog bed followed by the patter of small toenails on the old linoleum. "Yes," I said. "I'll be fine. The Police said the locks were good. I'll have a quick snack, set my laptop up, and do some work. I'm a book editor."

John looked as though he was trying not to grin again.

I stopped myself from saying 'what' in the nick of time.

"No Wi-Fi. She told me a while ago she didn't have a computer."

I groaned. "So I'll have to go back home if I need the internet? Which I will of course. I was hoping for some time away from my boring brother. I can't leave these dogs alone for hours on end, either."

He sat there yawning, and did a slow and mesmerizing stretch which hollowed his belly, expanded his chest, and made his biceps bulge quite beautifully as he shoved his hands back through his mane of nearly dry hair. "Come to the pub and make use of ours. You can set up in the court-yard with the dogs, and if it gets too busy we can tie them up out back with mine. I'll tell them not to eat yours."

Then he rose from the chair. I couldn't look him in the eye for longer that a second or two after that display. "Thank you," I managed. "Yes, maybe."

Yes *of course,* screamed my long-neglected body.

3

THE POLICE COME CALLING

IT WAS no surprise when early the next morning I received a call from a gruff-voiced person who introduced himself as DS Bruce Carver. Could he come out and ask me a few more questions? I graciously agreed through a storm of yapping. In fact I was bursting to know what they'd discovered so far, although far from certain they'd tell me anything.

I shooed the dogs out, refueled them when they re-appeared, and dived into the old-fashioned but functional shower.

It was a relief to be awake. All night long I'd twisted and turned in the spare bedroom, listening to the waves crashing on the nearby shore, and trying to discourage the dogs from sharing my bed. Isobel's dead eyes and the blood on the carpet had swirled around in my brain all mixed up with John's naked chest and American aggression and Paul's excellent legs and BBC voice. The dreams had been both erotic and horrifying. By the time I crawled out from under the floral bedcover there were bags under my eyes and itchy bites around my ankles – maybe there'd been sandflies in the garden the evening before? Surely there weren't fleas in the old house? But the dogs showed no signs of being bitten so I calmed down about that after a few minutes.

I did my best with a clean T-shirt and some make-up and was ready for DS Carver in the nick of time. He slid out of a charmless grey sedan he'd parked beside my Ford Focus and introduced me to his off-sider, Detective Marion Wick. I led them into Isobel's sitting room and we settled into armchairs with Sanderson linen slip-covers – very floral, and on their last legs in places.

DS Carver wore a dark suit, had severely bitten finger-nails, and rather a lot of cologne. Maybe it would wear off later in the day? Detective Wick was very slim and had the most amazing eyes – huge and dark as though they'd been computer-enhanced. She said she'd be recording the interview. I nodded. I'd presumed they would be.

"So," DS Carver began, looming so far forward I was engulfed in a cloud of double strength cologne. "Walk us through the scene in the church again if you don't mind..."

I tried to smother a cough. Holy Moly, did the man bathe in the stuff? I leaned well back in my chair. "I'm not really a witness to anything except finding her," I objected. "But okay," I took a deep breath. Oh golly, that was awful cologne. "I went in to the village to put a notice up on the community board outside the church –"

"What time was this?" DS Carver barked.

"Around ten? Mid-morning. I'm really not sure." From the look on his pinched face it seemed he didn't like my answer. Well, tough. I hadn't expected events to unfold the way they did so I hadn't noted the time. "You can check that with the emergency phone service," I added. "We called them the minute we found her."

He waved a hand, which I took to be a signal to continue.

"I spoke with the vicar for a couple of minutes. He was painting the top of the church fence. I teased him about the carnation tucked into the band of his hat. He said Isobel Crombie had given it to him when she came to freshen up the church flowers."

"And?" Detective Wick asked, crossing her long, slender legs.

"He said she'd been inside the church for quite a long time."

"Did he seem edgy?" Carver demanded.

"Not really."

I was starting to feel like a criminal with all his questions, so decided to try some yoga breathing.

"Did you expect she'd been injured?"

I inhaled slowly and tried to stare him down. "No, of course not. Why would I? She was just a little old lady I'd seen around the village. I didn't know her." The room became quiet. "Would you like tea or coffee?" I asked into the humming silence.

They both shook their heads.

"What happened next?" Detective Wick asked.

"We went into the church and found her. The vicar took her pulse. Or tried to. No pulse. And not breathing, because he checked with the mirror from my handbag. He seemed to know what to do. He said he'd been a chaplain in Afghanistan, so I guess he was familiar with blood. Unfortunately."

She widened her huge eyes, and DS Carver gnawed on his bottom lip for a few seconds.

It seemed to be up to me to continue. "I phoned for an ambulance and the Police, the vicar said a prayer, and then he..." I stopped, because DS Carver had held up a hand as though he was directing traffic.

"He *said a prayer?*"

"He's a man of God. Why wouldn't he?" It had seemed fair enough to me. "And while he was down there praying he had a good look under her head and said it wouldn't be a gunshot wound. Which I guess he probably also knows a bit about."

"How long did all of this take?" Detective Wick asked.

I shrugged. "A couple of minutes? No time at all. We found her, we panicked for a moment in case anyone else was still there, then I phoned, and the vicar went out the back to check the other entrance in case they could have gone in or out that way."

Carver steepled his fingers, which displayed his nasty nails. "So you didn't have him in your sight the whole time? Could he have let someone out?"

"No, of course not! Well, he *could* have I suppose, but I'm sure he didn't."

"But would you have heard him, if you were on the phone?" Detective Wick queried. "You'd have been listening to the operator and answering questions by then, I imagine?"

I nodded at that. Couldn't argue. I certainly hadn't been concentrating on what Paul was doing – not that I'd expected he'd done anything other than a quick recce. And thinking back, had I still been on the phone? I knew I hadn't got up from the pew, anyway.

I bent and scratched my itchy ankle. "It's not a very big church. I've never been out the back but I doubt there are more than one or two little rooms. I don't recall hearing any doors opening or closing."

"Moving on," Carver snapped, sending me a glare as sharp as his name.

I was still worried I'd somehow incriminated Paul. "He was back very fast," I muttered. "And then the two constables arrived and I'm sure they've told you the rest."

I thought for a few seconds, and my tummy felt squelchy. It couldn't have been Paul, could it? There was nothing to say he hadn't murdered her earlier and then come out to do his fence-painting as though nothing was wrong. Although why would he? I decided that made no sense at all.

"Did you know Miss Crombie well?"

I shuffled around in my chair a bit. There was a spring doing a bit of a poke under the fabric. "No – not at all. I already told you that."

"So why are you here?" Detective Wick asked.

I tried to look casual and hoped it didn't come across as shifty instead. "Total chance. The notice I'd put up was for a house minding and pet feeding service I operate." (Okay, that sounded a bit grand, but I'd give a lot to be slimmer and to have eyes like hers.) "And when Miss Crombie's sister came into the church to see her sister, she said she and her husband were going on a cruise and started panicking about who would look after Isobel's dogs. So..."

"Hang on... hang on," DS Carver interrupted. "Let's backtrack a bit. Why was she at the church?"

I took a deep breath and immediately regretted the cologne again. Didn't the uniformed and plain-clothes cops talk to each other?

"*Because*," I said, trying not to sound as though I was explaining simple arithmetic to five year olds, "She was also on the flower roster. The vicar had her number in his phone. He offered to tell her about her sister, and the lady policeman said she hated informing relatives, and sounded grateful if they could do it together. So the vicar phoned – the sister's name is Mrs Alsop, which you no doubt know by now – and it turned out she was just across the road at the shops. So she tore over while I was still there."

DS Carver looked daggers at me for a few seconds. "Talk about irregular," he muttered.

How was this *my* fault?

I liked Marion Wick better, so I said to her, "And the sister was shocked, of course, and blurted it out about the cruise and the dogs. And the vicar asked if I'd be free to look after the dogs and the cottage while they were away because he'd seen my notice. And I was. So here I am."

I wasn't getting anything from them in return so I casually asked if they'd be investigating the sister's husband.

Carver's eyes sharpened even further if that was possible. "Why?"

I tried to stare him down, but it wasn't easy. "He's a bit of a flash Harry. The sort of person who puts people's backs up. Or so I've heard."

"Who from?"

It was my turn to wave a languid hand. I wasn't keen to drop Bon Jovi in the mire, so I said, "No-one in particular. Just local rumor. Bills being paid late. Money owed for too long. That sort of thing. There might be nothing to it."

Marion Wick promptly started scrolling through her cell phone. "Alsop A-One Autos," she said to DS Carver after a few seconds. "Three branches. They import top-of-the-line used vehicles, mostly from Europe."

"You'll have to hurry if you want to talk to him," I said. "They're going off on this cruising holiday later today, I think."

Carver grimaced. "Right. Don't leave town, Ms Summerfield."

"What?" I exclaimed, as my stomach did a huge surging bounce.

"Figure of speech," he added, rising from his chair with

the merest ghost of a grin. "But I presume we'll be able to find you here if we need to ask anything further?"

"Not necessarily." He'd given me a real fright with his 'don't leave town' so I didn't feel like groveling with helpfulness.

"So how can we contact you?" Detective Wick asked in a much softer tone. "May I have your cell number please?"

I recited it for her and she tapped it into hers.

"I'll either be here or at home in Drizzle Bay or at the Burkeville Bar and Grill," I added. "There's no Wi-Fi here and I need it for my editing work."

"Why go as far as Burkeville?" she asked, sliding her phone into a pocket of her jacket.

I decided that was really none of her business, and I'd had enough of her skinny body and long legs and huge eyes. It was time to stand up for slightly older, curvier women!

"I know the owner," I said sweetly. "John has a lovely outdoor courtyard area and good Wi-Fi. He's invited me to bring the dogs and work there when I wanted to."

Her eyebrows drew together. "He knows you're living here – alone?"

Oh for heaven's sake... I didn't want to get into half-naked surfing and cups of tea at sunset. I probably should have, but hoping it wouldn't come back to bite me on the bum I simply nodded and tried to look mysterious.

"Riiiight..." she said on a long exhale. "John." I wondered what she meant by that as the dogs and I led them to the gate. It sounded as though she knew him. Not in a personal capacity, I hoped.

Then, public duty done, I decided to have a proper prowl around Isobel's property before setting off to the Burkeville Bar and Grill. I hadn't seen much of the garden the previous evening, having been scared half out of my wits by John's sudden and silent arrival up the cliff path.

There proved to be quite a lot of land – maybe half an acre – with the old separate garage, a garden shed, the fruit and vegie plot close to the house, extensive flower borders and a big bumpy lawn that ended in rough beachy vegetation. The plot dived down the small incline toward the ocean, and apart from the piece of front fence with the gate there was only saggy post-and-wire farm fencing around the other boundaries. The dogs must have been trained to stick close to home because they could easily have squeezed their way through that. In fact everything was threadbare and run-down and needed paint or repairs. Plainly Isobel lived on the smell of an oily rag, unlike her bejeweled sister, but someone had to be helping her keep this much garden up to scratch. Maybe she traded labor for vegies?

I picked my way down to the damp, hard-packed sand for a few minutes' walk. After scrambling through yellow lupins and lots of that low-growing sand coprosma with all the crazy tangled twigs, the teddies and I made good progress. Itsy clamped his little teeth around a smooth grey stick of driftwood and proudly carried it with him. Fluffy made half-hearted attempts to share it but was warned off with fierce growls and had to find a stick of his own. Or *her* own? I knew there was one of each, but wasn't entirely sure yet who was who.

The tide was way out. No waves for John. Which reminded me I should be sitting at the Burkeville, trying to get some work done.

As I strode along, I decided to swing by the Alsops' home after that to see how extreme the comparison was between Isobel and Margaret's houses. Maybe it was a case of the spinster sister being expected to look after the parents, who must have been pretty elderly because Isobel had to have been around seventy. That would make sense. *Everything* here was old – older in many ways than I'd expect for someone of her age. Those awful armchairs in the sitting room... the barely serviceable bed-linens... the ancient gas-stove... the lack of a computer. Had she been trapped here with them? It was easy to think so.

So why on earth would anyone kill her? She didn't appear to have two pennies to rub together.

Did she really own the old cottage? Maybe it had been left to both sisters jointly on the death of their parents? Was poor old Isobel unable to progress her life at all? And if so, did John know? Maybe she hadn't been free to sell it to him? I'd definitely be asking about that when I saw him a little later.

Conversely, was Margaret sick of waiting to inherit it? No – terrible thought! They were sisters. She wouldn't have killed Isobel to get it. Would she?

I could ask Paul McCreagh. He seemed to have his finger on the pulse of his parishioners, dead and alive. And there was always my brother, lawyer Graham. Older than me, staid and rule-bound. The soul of discretion. But he might slip his baby sister a tiny morsel of information about one of his clients. Just a sliver. Like did Isobel own her home outright?

There was probably some sort on online register of home-owners, too. I'd have a look once I was comfortably settled at John's, dogs tied to my chair-legs, flat white and Danish pastry waiting to be enjoyed, with the world at my fingertips again.

I heaved a deep sigh and turned back. It would have been nice to walk further but I hadn't locked the cottage up. Not that there was a living soul in sight to steal anything – or much to steal. The sheep on Jim Drizzle's nearby farm added the odd 'baaa' to the gentle wash of the waves, and something that sounded like a tree-shredder roared away intermittently, but that was it.

———

THIS TIME I took the right road. Drizzle *Bay* Road and not Drizzle *Beach* Road. It was a much shorter trip. Past the big brick gateposts of Drizzle Farm where someone was indeed forcing branches down a shredder. I slowed for a few seconds and gave Lord Drizzle a wave. The actual labor was being done by a stringy youth in droopy jeans. Then I passed Lisa the vet's old house and clinic. Lisa often pours out her troubles to me when she's treating the animals at the shelter where I volunteer as a dog walker. Most of her troubles are to do with her ex-husband, Ten Ton – a mountain of a man who's as tall and broad as she is short and slim. How they ever got together is a mystery, but they produced three children before they split up, so they must have been okay once. And in no time I'd reached the village outskirts. Mindful I was looking fairly casual I ducked into home, changed my shoes, and swapped my jeans for a skirt. I was onto the main road and then the new expressway only minutes later.

"So," John said as I arrived with my laptop in one hand and pink and blue leashes in the other. The little white teddies bounced around, enjoying somewhere new to explore. No doubt their doggie perfume drifted sideways because bone-shaking barks soon rent the air from somewhere behind the back fence. Itsy and Fluffy seriously tried to sound intimidating in return.

"Cool it!" John yelled, and Fire and Ice did.

"Quiet, darlings," I implored the teddies. This had no effect at all, but it did earn me an eyebrow lift and a glance of total amusement from John's startling blue eyes.

"They're not mine," I protested. "I need to earn my authority yet."

He bent. He placed a forefinger on each nose. The dogs both went cross-eyed. "Shut it," he said softly, keeping his fingers there. Itsy and Fluffy's noses twitched, sampling the smell of this stranger who dared to try and control them, but they held still and quiet.

What would I do if John tried something like that on me? Probably cave right in. He'd said he was used to getting things done, and I was kind of hoping I might be one of the things he'd like to get done. Unless he was already getting PC Wick done, which would really get on *my* wick.

Within a couple more minutes John had me organized. Me in a chair in the shade so I could see my screen. Itsy and Fluffy tied to a table leg so they could choose sun or shade according to their taste. Me with a flat white, him with a pineapple juice, and his dad, Erik, skulking around sending us suspicious glances.

Suspicion seemed to lurk in the family. John had been full of suspicion the previous evening. He'd thought maybe I'd bought Isobel's house out from under him. Or that perhaps she'd left it to the church. Then he'd assumed the house had been broken into when he saw the fingerprint powder (which I suppose was fair enough.) He didn't seem to believe the vicar had been in Afghanistan. Didn't believe Tom Alsop was necessarily honest.

He probably didn't believe I was there to look after the dogs, either.

I have to say although I'd enjoyed the surfer version of him with all the flowing hair, the tidied-up-for-work edition was almost better. Long legs in black jeans, grey T-shirt stretched snugly around his big shoulders and chest, and his hair pulled back and wound up. I could see now that the sides of his head were shaved almost down to his scalp. The blond bristles of his undercut shone in the sun. If he hadn't had that, his mop of hair would have been even more spectacular. And what girl doesn't enjoy running her fingers through a decent head of masculine waves?

Erik the dad was something else. Not quite as tall. More heavily built, although most of it looked like muscle. And with a shock of short, pure white hair that seemed at odds with his alert dark eyes and unlined face. I assumed John was closing in on forty, so Erik must be sixtyish, minimum. He looked sensational for that, despite the old-man hair.

"I've just had the Police at the cottage," I said once Erik was busy with the hissing coffee machine. I'm sure John sat up a little straighter.

"Any theories? Do they know who killed her?"

"Not that they'd tell *me*. And I'm sure they wouldn't keep running over the same facts if they did." I looked at him very closely as I added, "I passed on your opinion of Tom Alsop being less than honest."

To his credit, not a muscle moved in his chiseled face. Maybe his hand tightened around his glass though – or maybe he'd been ready to lift it for another sip. I watched as his mouth pursed around the rim. Imagined what it would feel like to kiss. Then wondered if Detective Wick had any first-hand experience of that.

He didn't even ask if I'd mentioned his name. To be honest I found that surprising. Wouldn't you want to know?

"Tom Alsop's a slime-ball," was all he said. And that was after a silent gap long enough for me to take a bite of my Danish and chew for a while.

He rose to his feet, leaving his half full glass on the table. A slime-ball? It sounded like he knew more that he'd told me the previous evening, and now it seemed I'd offended him and he'd sloped off. I took another bite.

He returned perhaps thirty seconds later, setting a small casserole of fresh water under the table for the dogs. "Don't kick it," he said. "Have fun. Lauren will get you anything else you want." He picked up his glass and disappeared for good. Huh! He was kind to the dogs, but didn't want any more of me.

I checked my emails and sent a few brief replies. Then got down to the current manuscript. Goodness, the poor woman had no idea. Who was telling the story? The ditzy heroine or the muscle-bound hero?

Occasionally both in the same paragraph.

Sometimes the hero's housekeeper got a look in, too – carefully explaining things in case we hadn't already got the point. This was going to take quite some time to work through. Never mind – money in the bank at the end of it.

After about twenty minutes my bottom had had enough of the hard metal chair. I pushed it back from the table and stretched, standing so I could flex my legs and clench my bum-cheeks together a few times. The dogs scrambled to their feet, instantly awake and ready for walkies, even though they'd been sound asleep and gently snoring seconds earlier.

"Lie down," I commanded. A lot of good that did.

"Right on time," Erik said, arriving with a cushion and a grin that showed a lot of teeth.

I must have cocked an eyebrow at him because he said, "Twenty minutes is about as long as most people can last in these chairs. So they stand up and stretch, and then think they may as well wander as far as the bar for another beer or coffee. Works almost every time."

I accepted the cushion with thanks. And pulled out my purse and ordered another flat white – to be delivered in fifteen minutes or so. I didn't want to end up so wired I couldn't sleep for another night.

"It's awn the house," he said, waving my money away. "I'll take it out of Jawn's wages." He flashed all those teeth as he strode off again. His accent sounded quite different to John's. Jawn versus Jaarn. Something for me to think about another time...

The shadows were moving with the sun. I shuffled around to the adjacent chair, taking my cushion with me and continuing with the ill-written romance I'd been paid to edit. But I was fooling myself if I thought I was here for anything except to see John. I'd be more comfortable at home in my own study. He'd disappeared and was showing no signs of coming back; should I ask Erik if he expected him to return anytime soon? No – that smacked of stalking and desperation so held my tongue. After drinking my second flat white and ordering a ham-and-cheese filled croissant 'to go' from Lauren, the pretty waitress who collected my cup, I closed the laptop, untangled the teddies, and set off to check out the Alsops' Drizzle Bay residence instead.

Stalking? Who – me?

———

As LUCK WOULD HAVE it I'd spotted their address on the list held to Isobel's fridge door with a Leaning Tower of Pisa magnet. Presumably a souvenir from her well-traveled sister.

Sandalwood Grove. It sounded expensive, and it certainly was. Holy Moly – six big houses that can't have been much more than a year old. The trees were all new, too, plainly trucked in after they'd grown at least twenty feet tall in some upmarket plant nursery. Everything was carefully positioned to preserve the ocean views. Tom and Margaret were definitely doing well for themselves.

Not an ideal neighborhood to be seen hanging about in, I reminded myself, so I snapped a couple of quick photos of their house for no good reason at all and then drove home. Our parents' old place was gracious enough, but bore all the marks of a lawn-mowing service instead of a family of keen gardeners. Things were... neat. It's just easier not to have flower beds with two enthusiastic spaniels dashing about. Graham had insisted they have as much room as possible to run free so apart from the driveway the land was all one big fenced area with a few trees around the edges. 'My' area was a terracotta pot either side of the garage door. Right now the pansies in them were at the 'dangling over the edge and not flowering much' stage.

Get something else for summer, Merry...

What was I going to do with the teddies for the next couple of hours? I needn't have worried. The moment I opened the gate the dogs did another big sniff at each other and showed no agro so I took the leads off the teddies and they all gamboled around in an excited pack, staged a few mock-attacks with no real savagery, and were soon having the time of their lives. The spaniels might have been bigger, but the teddies were really fast. I left the door to the kitchen open in case anyone wanted to bolt in to safety.

Right – a cup of jasmine and mango tea to go with my croissant! Then I settled down to work for another couple of hours without the distraction of an athletic American hovering anywhere nearby. Or indeed, not hovering. I kept comparing poor Isobel's disintegrating cottage to her sister's gross but no doubt glorious mansion. If Graham and I had been living in such unequal circumstances I'd have been hopping mad. Probably mad enough to point out that the sibling with all the advantages should be kind enough to even things up somewhat.

In Isobel's case might she have demanded Margaret slip her poor dutiful sister some cash for looking after the old parents? (If indeed that was the situation, and if she was expected to share the eventual house sale proceeds with wealthy Margaret.) Could she have tried blackmail? Would that be enough to set either of the Alsops off on a murderous rampage?

I let out a frustrated groan. A rampage sounded like multiple murders and there was only one, thank heavens. And really – what might she have known she could blackmail them for? Being a mean sister wouldn't be enough.

I needed Graham to come home, relax with his predictable Scotch on the rocks, and lose his customary caution. Then I could start the process of getting him to spill the details about who owned the old cottage and who stood to benefit. Sadly though, tonight was his Rotary meeting and he'd be off with the cream of the local business world discussing projects that might improve the district. I'd have to phone him from Isobel's once he was home because I knew disturbing him at work would get me nowhere.

4

LURLINE AND LISA

AT FOUR-THIRTY I closed my laptop. I'd wrangled the reluctant lovers into better shape – or at least given the hopeful author plenty to think about – so I clipped the leads onto the teddies' collars again, bundled them into the car, and headed for the Drizzle Bay Animal Shelter. That's a very hopeful description for the large sunny shed behind Lurline Lawrence's old house, but it's what the brown and gold sign on the front fence says. Someone had taken a Sharpie to the sign since I'd last been there and drawn mustaches on the cat and dog. I couldn't help but smirk, even though it was total vandalism. The cat now looked rather like Hercule Poirot from the TV programs.

Mindful it was a warmish day and that pets shouldn't be left in cars, the three of us trotted up the side path, two of us with hairy white legs going a mile a minute, one of us with lightly tanned legs strolling much more slowly in the high-heeled red sandals I'd put on to impress John. Fat chance that had worked! The door to the animal shelter was open so we walked in.

Lurline was attempting to clip the knots out of a large and snarly Persian. The poor cat was trussed up in the loops of a dog grooming table and wasn't enjoying the process. To judge from Lurline's flushed face and pinched mouth, neither was she. A sudden storm of yaps from the teddies as they scented prey did nothing to help the situation.

The cat increased its hissing and struggling, doing its best to escape from the harness.

Lurline glanced sideways at the excited Bichons and yelled, "Get them out, for heaven's sake!"

I was trying to! Small dogs who weigh no more than cats can get very heavy when they're determined. Finally I managed to drag them, protesting and lunging back on their leads, out into the garden. There was a timber seat at the far end, so I staggered across the bumpy lawn toward it, avoiding the patches where a rabbit hutch had plainly been because the grass was nibbled down to nothing, and sprinklings of tiny turds remained. The rabbit in question – an enormous grey thing – dived into the straw-filled bedroom end of the hutch, now positioned under a tree dripping with small green peaches. I clung onto the teddy's leads with grim determination to get them away from the rabbit droppings and they finally went off the boil.

Phew – this pet-minding was really taking it out of me. I

sat and recovered in the sun for a few minutes until Lurline appeared.

"Lovely to see you," she called, bustling across the lawn. Her face was still red with exertion, and her patchwork skirt swirled and flapped around her ankles. "Poor old Prince Albert," she added. "Someone who had better remain nameless reported him squeezing through their cat door and pinching their own cat's food. No mention of the sad condition he was in, and no concern that maybe the owner was in bad health and couldn't care for him properly." She rolled her big brown eyes. "*Some people!*" Her indignation practically exploded out of her ears.

I watched as she began to pat the teddies. "So who does the cat belong to?" I asked. "You're right he's in a sad condition."

"How can anyone see an animal like that and not do something?" Lurline demanded. "Old Rona Jarvis in Beach Street, as it happens. I recognized the name Prince Albert when they said he'd snagged his name-tag on something outside their cat door. He won Best in Show a couple of years ago at the Drizzle Bay Summer Festival. You wouldn't think that to look at him now."

"And how's old Rona?" I asked, thinking privately of not-much-younger Isobel, who'd also lived alone with only pets for company.

"I went to check," Lurline said, switching her attention from Itsy to Fluffy, or possibly from Fluffy to Itsy. The little dogs stood braced, black eyes twinkling, loving it. "Probably got Alzheimer's. Half-starved and senile, anyway. I got hold of Social Services and they've arranged Meals on Wheels and a regular agency helper for an hour twice a week. Not fantastic, but it's a start. Catching the cat was a lot harder."

"You do wonders," I murmured, because it was true. Lurline looks like a hippie who never escaped from the sixties but she has a heart as big as Texas and her kindness extends to people as well as animals. "I hate to tell you what I'm here for," I added. "But I don't think I can do any more dog-walking for you for a while – unless you have someone the size of these two."

Not very likely. The dogs that end up needing Lurline's care tend toward too large and too hungry for the average home; cute puppies for Christmas who grow into unwelcome out-of-control destruction specialists.

She shook her head. "No-one small. Are you looking after them?"

"Pet-sitting. Out at Isobel Crombie's cottage at The Point." I waited for the reaction, and sure enough…

"She was killed, wasn't she!" Lurline exclaimed.

"Awful thing to happen to a harmless old biddy like her," I said.

"Not so harmless," Lurline surprised me by saying. "She looked as though butter wouldn't melt in her mouth but she had fingers in strange pies, believe me."

Huh? I looked at her more sharply. "What sort of pies?"

Lurline shrugged. "You hear things," she muttered.

That pulled me up short. What sort of 'strange pies'

could possibly be accessible in sleepy Drizzle Bay? "She can't have deserved what happened, though?" I asked.

Lurline didn't seem to mind me being nosy, and I'd walked dogs for her for ages now, so we were on good terms. She repeated the shrug. "She did the tax returns for a number of people in the Bay – and further afield. She knew a lot. I heard she put money into all sorts of things because she got the inside skinny on stuff."

No way ho-zay!

"I doubt it, Lurline. Honestly, the house is threadbare. The comparison between her sister's place and that decrepit cottage has to be seen to be believed."

"Margaret Alsop's her sister – right? Putting up a fancy front, I reckon." She shook her head and her dreadlocks bounced around her shoulders. "And maybe the old cottage was a front of the opposite kind. Purposely run-down looking. As though Isobel didn't want anyone suspecting it was worth burgling. It would have looked like easy pickings, being so isolated. One elderly lady, two tiny dogs. Maybe the well-worn clothes and ancient car were supposed to indicate there was nothing worth having." She raised an eyebrow. "But how large is her bank balance? What's she got hidden there?"

Now it was my turn to shake my head. "There's not even any Wi-Fi out at The Point. Did she have an office in the village somewhere?"

Lurline narrowed her eyes. "Must have done. Never

heard of one." Then she surprised me by saying, "You were there when they found her, weren't you?"

Wheee! News travels fast in a small place like Drizzle Bay.

I nodded. "Would rather not have been. It was horrible."

She nodded with sympathy but wasn't going to leave it alone. "In the church? Who'd do it there?"

"No doubt the Police will discover who," I said, thinking of this morning's visit from Carver and Wick. "The vicar and I found her lying in the aisle amongst all the flowers she'd brought with her to arrange. Looking quite peaceful until we saw the blood leaking from the back of her head."

That wasn't really true. Her eyes had been staring – wide open and distressed. Her unlipsticked mouth was strangely twisted. One open hand had landed on her thigh and might have been reaching up for help. I shivered, picturing her again.

"Crikey," Lurline muttered, glancing down at Itsy and Fluffy. "You want to know you've put the wrong colored leads on these two?"

"Um... how?" I asked, welcoming the diversion. I was still trying to sort them out.

Lurline had no such qualms. She upended one of the teddies, who gave a surprised bark. "Little boy," she said. She grabbed the other and positioned its nether regions a bit too close to my face for comfort. "Little girl."

I reared back. "Yes, I knew there was one of each," I agreed. "But the names on their tags aren't much help, and …

things are covered in fur. Graham's spaniels are both boys."
To my relief she lowered the 'little girl' to the grass again.

"Gold for a girl, silver for sir," she said with a grin, touching the tags hanging from their collars.

That made it easier, but I felt sorry for Fluffy. "So Itsy's the girl? What kind of a name is 'Fluffy' for a male dog?"

"Not exactly male any longer. No worries there." She bent and resumed petting their upturned heads and they instantly forgave her for the indignity of being flipped over and inspected. She sent me a sideways glance. "Poor old Miss Crombie – murdered in the aisle."

"Presumably so," I said. "Unlikely anyone could have done it elsewhere and then carried her into the church. The vicar was painting the fence outside."

Talk about obvious... Paul might not have noticed a stranger (or not a stranger) popping in for a few moments of quiet contemplation, but if they'd been carrying a limp and bleeding body in their arms he certainly would have. He also might not have noticed them quietly leaving because I guess it's the kind of place people drift in and out of without always wanting to chat. If the back door of the church was locked then they had to come out through the lovely old double doors at the front. Which had definitely been open. Open to welcome anyone who wished to enter, and therefore easy to leave through again. I remembered Paul closing them later to give Margaret some privacy.

I clutched my suddenly queasy tummy. The murderer might have been at work right when I was inappropriately admiring Paul's legs. Or as we chatted about the prospects of pet-sitting jobs over by the notice board.

Oh get real, Merry! Paul had said Isobel had been inside the church 'for quite a while' and I also remembered him saying it wasn't worth trying rescue breathing because he could tell from the state of the bleeding and the lack of pulse she was definitely dead and had been so for ages. Well, for long enough that he couldn't revive her, anyway.

I dragged my attention back to Lurline. "Seriously though – what have you heard about the 'strange pies' she might have had her fingers in? I didn't really know her. It's very odd living in her house amongst all her stuff. I only ended up doing it because her sister was going away on a cruise and didn't have time to arrange anything better. I just happened to be Johnny on the spot."

Lurline sniffed. "That figures. Margaret Alsop thinks she's the bee's knees, but that car-yard husband of hers pulls the strings in the marriage. He says 'jump' and she asks 'how high?' I'll bet the cruise was his idea – one more thing to try and impress people with. And you can't tell me his car business is entirely legit. Have you noticed how many foreign people are associated with it?"

I shook my head. "I don't have the same opportunities as you to be out and about. I'm staring at my screen half the day."

"Out and about," Lurline murmured. "Well, that's one way to describe rescuing mistreated animals and looking after them."

"Mmmm, sorry – foot in my mouth," I agreed. "I meant you have the chance to see a lot more of the community than I do. That's partly why I've taken on the house-and-pet minding. I'm sick of being stuck in the same place, mostly with only Graham for company."

She was quick to forgive my description of the amazing work she does. "Foreign people," she repeated. "The car salespeople, the mechanics I've seen, even the office staff. Indian people and Chinese people and Germans, too. Or people who sound very German, anyway. And they're never the same ones."

I raised an eyebrow. "How can you tell?"

She stared off into the distance, lifted one of her dreadlocks and brushed it to and fro across her lips as she considered. "I always see people as animals," she said after a few seconds. "The woman who looks like a poodle – all curls and long nose. The man who looks like a walrus – big mustache and leaky eyes. The crocodile lady with too many teeth. The oily-looking chap who's skinny as a snake... Huh! I didn't really think about that until you asked. But yes, the animals change, so the people must be changing too."

"And you think something shady's going on?"

"Hiya, girls!" came a sudden cheerful greeting from the other end of the garden. We both swiveled our heads in that direction. Lisa Smedley the vet is a tiny thing but she has a voice that carries easily across farm paddocks or sports fields.

"Lisa!" we exclaimed in unison, and with real pleasure,

too. The teddies set up a huge ruckus, bouncing around and tugging at their leads. I was unsure whether they were pleased to see her or remembered past appointments at her vet clinic.

Lisa sat on the seat with me after Lurline moved aside and perched on a low wall nearby.

"Just the person I need," Lurline said, folding her skirt around her knees. "I've got someone for you. Persian cat, full of knots, poor thing. Beyond me, I think."

"Needs sedating?" Lisa suggested, clicking her tongue at the Bichons, which made them bark even harder. From somewhere out of sight several other dogs with much deeper voices joined in.

"Probably," Lurline agreed. "I got the poor thing back into a cage because it wasn't going well."

"I walked in with these two," I said. "Total pandemonium."

Lisa grinned at me and then down at the teddies. "You've got the wrong leads on them. Isobel Crombie's dogs – I wondered what had become of them."

"Pet-sitting," I said, wanting to get back to the 'strange pies'. "What do you know about her?"

Lisa looked non-committal. "Nice enough little woman. Kind to her pets. Always paid right away – never had to chase her for money."

And then Lurline, bless her, said, "I always thought there was something shady about her."

"Well, there must have been, mustn't there?" Lisa agreed.

"Murdered, and in the church. That's not a random sort of thing. That's intentional. So why do you reckon?"

"No good asking me," I said. "I've seen her around the village but never up close. Don't think I'd ever spoken with her."

"She was good with money," Lurline insisted. "Never looked as though she had any, but I heard she was clever with investments and getting in on the ground floor with new businesses."

Lisa nodded. "Like the whale watching trips and that expensive new gallery? How does that survive, do you think? I wouldn't have thought there were many people in Drizzle Bay who can afford their prices, but they must have been open for at least a year now."

"The whales are wonderful," I said. "Ideal to bring some tourists to the area, although I don't expect they'll be buying pricey art."

"It's not a huge boat like the ones they have down at Kaikoura," Lisa mused. "Brett Royal can't take more than a dozen or fifteen people out at a time."

"Maybe he brings them in?" Lurline suggested.

We both looked at her in astonishment. "What – people smuggling?" Lisa asked.

"Or drugs. His boat's big enough to meet other vessels out past the horizon and do midnight transfers. Who'd suspect him? Smiley, easy-going Brett?"

"I don't *think* so," I said. She'd shocked me. "Anyway, how would Isobel have made money out of that?"

Lisa tapped her chin. A slight smile danced about her lips. "Did the money laundering for him? Hid the funds? Arranged currency transfers?" Then she shook her head. "This is terrible – assassinating the character of a nice little woman just because someone killed her. Forget I ever suggested that. I came to have a groan about Ten Ton, actually."

"What's the big lump done now?" Lurline asked. But it was asked affectionately enough. Lisa's estranged husband, Ten Ton Smedley, is our local mechanic, and despite having what looks like an ever-changing line of vehicles to service outside his workshop he never seems to have enough spare cash to pay any extra to Lisa. Or perhaps he's simply not willing to subsidize her possibly quite good vet's income.

"All the kids need new sports shoes," Lisa said. "Good ones. Expensive ones. Not rubbish. They're putting their hearts and souls into their training. Bailey's playing inter-club tennis and she's *good*. Mac's made it into the college's first eleven for cricket. Also good. And Pete's taken up archery of all things. I don't think he needs special shoes but if the others are getting them he'd better have new sneakers to keep things fair. He's so accurate it's scary."

"Better send him out spear-fishing for dinner, then?" Lurline suggested.

We got the giggles at that. Pete's no more than twelve, so hardly likely to be let loose on his own with a deadly weapon.

Lisa sighed. "I'm serious, though. They're his kids. He

should be willing to pay an extra whack for things like this. He should be showing he's proud of them."

Lurline and I both nodded.

"I hear he always has enough cash to drink at the Burkeville," she added. "No buying a box of whatever's on special at the supermarket for him."

"Maybe he's lonely?" I suggested. "You have all your cows and horses and farmers and pet-owners to interact with. Who does he have? People who're annoyed about having to get their cars serviced."

"He could come and live at home again," Lisa said acidly. "We'd talk to him. In fact the kids would never stop."

"Might be why he stays away?" Lurline said, smiling to take the sting from her comment. "Cuppa?"

"Yes please," we chorused.

We ambled inside together after I'd tied the teddies to the end of the seat. They settled down in the shade underneath it with long-suffering sighs.

"Okay," I said, unwilling to let go the subject of Isobel Crombie's possible expertise with money. "What's the gallery doing she can grab a piece of?"

Lurline thought for a few moments. "Maybe they're fencing stolen art," she said. "And she's blackmailing them to keep it secret?"

"You're good at this," I said as Lisa and I leaned on the kitchen counter and Lurline took three mugs from the hooks under her kitchen canister shelf.

But smartly dressed Winston Bamber? He of the

constant cravat? I couldn't see it. Mind you, I also couldn't see the residents of Drizzle Bay parting with a thousand bucks for his large pastel-colored canvasses with bands of paint splatter on them. Or the expensive, useless, narrow-necked pottery bottles in lurid colors. Or the metallic-painted wooden trays with notices warning they 'were not functional items and intended only as wall art.' He had one with the most amazing copper and gold banding I'd been admiring, but not at the eye-watering price on the discreet attached tag.

"Not very likely," I said. "Winnie's an old sweetie, and pretty conventional. I don't think he'd be willing to risk his reputation but I can't imagine how he stays in business."

"Yeah, probably right," Lisa agreed. "Not blackmail, then. Maybe he won Lotto."

"Maybe Isobel did, too," I said. "But she hasn't any visible money." I elbowed Lurline now we were standing side by side. "Why do you think she has?"

"Someone killed her for something," she replied. "It wasn't for sex. It probably wasn't for drugs. So that leaves money, eh?" She turned the tap fill the kettle for tea.

———

EVENTUALLY LURLINE GATHERED up our empty mugs. Lisa glanced at her watch and gave a guilty curse, and I went to untie the teddies. I held them back until she had Prince Albert's cage stowed in her wagon and then I took them home. To their home. Isobel's home. My home for the fore-seeable future.

Finally on my own, I decided to have a thorough search through the rambling old place to see if I could substantiate any of Lurline's suspicions. I fed the teds, then chased them outside for a run-around. It wasn't long before they rattled back in through the dog door and curled up in the dotty dog bed after their day's excitement. By then I'd made sure both doors to the house were locked and was on my knees checking shelves and quietly opening drawers and cupboards in the kitchen. Nothing, nothing, nothing. Itsy came and dangled her gold tag into the bottom drawer when I opened it, but after a sniff at the muffin pans and cake tins and a snort of disappointment she went back to bed.

I moved to the sitting room. Plenty of books on gardening and flower arrangement – very well thumbed or else bought second hand. In the bedroom that had plainly been Isobel's there were faded nightgowns, uninspired undergarments, and neat but neutral clothes. I felt terrible going through all her things but surely the Police had already had a look if they wanted to? Cards from Christmases past had been bundled up with rubber bands and stowed in the bottom drawer of a bedside cabinet.

They were about the most personal thing I found. This was crazy – there had to be documents in her life. She had a gas stove. There must be a gas bill. With no computer she couldn't be paying online.

Then, finally, on the lowest shelf of the airing cupboard, I spotted an old cardboard box. It was partly hidden by some re-hemmed towels but maybe whoever had searched the place earlier had pushed them over to that side of the shelf? (If the Police ever searched people's airing cupboards? It seemed unlikely.)

Oh come *on*, Isobel! One old school exercise book? A year per page? I thumbed through in disbelief. Handwriting so neat you'd almost call it copperplate. Every gas bill and electricity bill and phone account was neatly detailed there, month by month, for years. The quarterly payments to the district council, the purchase of the Mini and its occasional servicing. The yearly insurances on house and property.

Then the handwriting changed to something a lot less tidy. A-ha! So old Mum or Dad had finally given Isobel the job of book-keeping? (Or she'd taken it over after they'd died.) A big spring-clip held a few invoices together but it was still a pretty sparse record, and that was everything the cardboard box contained. I wasn't buying it. There had to be more. Graham kept enormous amounts of paper filed at home, even though he paid most things online. Not very trusting, my brother!

Having checked everywhere likely for a desk, I thought about the garage. Might she have an old filing cabinet out there?

I'd no sooner decided to have a look when there was a knock on the kitchen door and a man's voice called out, "Merry, it's me, Paul."

5

THE CALM BEFORE THE STORM

THE DOGS immediately set up a huge yappy ruckus. Phew – lucky escape. A few minutes earlier and he'd have caught me nosily searching. I gave my hair a pat and smacked my cheeks a couple of times to give them some roses as I headed toward his voice. No time for lipstick.

He was looking a lot more vicarish today in dark slacks and a black shirt with a white dog collar at the neck. His sleeves were rolled back though, and his dark wavy hair was ruffled by the wind. He was, in a word or three, one hot vicar.

"Paul," I said, pulling the door open further.

"I hope I didn't give you a shock. I thought I'd better yell out to let you know it was only me."

"I'm amazed the dogs didn't hear you earlier." I led him into the kitchen through a sea of bouncy white barkers. "They should be tuckered out. I took them home and let them run around with Graham's spaniels most of the afternoon."

He bent and patted them both before settling himself in the chair I indicated.

"I parked out on the road," he said. "They probably didn't hear the car over the breakers. There's a big sea running again. It's clouding over, too."

Immediately I imagined John welded to his surfboard, hair flying, rushing down the terrifying edge of a huge wave. My heart did a bit of a lurch and my thighs might have trembled. Okay, definitely trembled. One hot vicar, one cool surfer. My cup runneth over.

"Are you okay with the cottage being so isolated?" Paul asked, hauling me back to reality. "I've been thinking it was probably a stupid thing to suggest. You living here with no-one else around. Woman on her own..." He looked embarrassed – and possibly a bit pink under his tan.

I thought again what a nice man he was. Quite a contrast to John who'd simply swaggered up out of the sea, barely clothed, and proceeded to be pretty direct until he spotted the fingerprint powder.

I smiled. "Isobel was a woman on her own. She was safe here, wasn't she?"

He sent me half a grin in return, and a nod. "She was less of a temptation, perhaps?"

"Paul, are you flirting?" I exclaimed.

He shook his head, but the grin didn't fade.

"No," I assured him. "I'm not worried about living here,

but it's always good to know someone has your safety in mind." I took the chair opposite. "How long had Isobel been here on her own? I've decided she probably looked after her parents for ages. And was a bit stuck as a result. There's not much money in evidence." Keen to keep him talking, I added, "Tea or coffee?"

Paul settled back. "Well, tea if you're boiling up. I don't want to steal your time. It's just a quick visit."

I stood and turned the tap on to fill the kettle. "It's okay – I worked a lot of the afternoon and got heaps done. Company's good. Did I guess right about her parents? Her sister looked so smart by comparison." I held up fingers as I said; "Less careworn. Much better dressed. And was going cruising. Quite a contrast."

I set yesterday's brown mug and floral teacup on the table and opened the pantry to search for teabags. Then I attempted the gas stove. "I don't suppose they've any idea yet who killed her, or why?"

Paul shook his head. "Not that I've heard. She'll be a loss to the church. She looked an unlikely Napoleon but she ruled the old-fashioned team of flower arranging ladies with a rod of iron. At all three churches. Here in Drizzle Bay, along in Burkeville, and out at Totara Flat."

That had me wrinkling my brow. "You have three churches?"

"They're hardly cathedrals, Merry. We spread the services around to suit each area. Only one a fortnight at Totara Flat, and we're lucky to get a dozen people, but the congregation enjoys knowing it's 'their' place of worship and 'their' grave-yard. There's a Sunday school as well in Burkeville, and sometimes we have weddings or funerals to cope with in each. Isobel bossed her team around with surprising compe-tence. We always had fresh flowers when and where we needed them."

"Good on her. So much nicer than the artificial ones. We all need projects to occupy us. I'd seen her pottering around the shops but never actually spoken to her."

And I'd certainly never seen her up close and as personal as she was when sprawled, dead and bleeding, on the church carpet. My strange brain went sideways and wondered if the stain had come out. Or maybe it had to be a left a while longer as evidence? Euw, no – surely not!

"She kept herself busy," Paul agreed. "Come tax time she was in demand for checking some of the local businesses' accounts and preparing their returns."

I raised an eyebrow, thinking of Lurline's suggestions. So maybe she'd been right after all? I hadn't expected that. Isobel had never struck me as anything but a sweet old spin-ster toddling by in the village. I wondered what she did with the extra money she made. She didn't spend it on clothes – that was for sure.

The kettle boiled and I poured the water over the teabags. "Weak or strong? Milk and sugar?"

Once our drinks we to our liking we sat either side of the table, sipping and gossiping. His arms were a bare two feet away as he leaned toward me, listening as I asked questions that were probably none of my business. Lovely strong arms. The tendons on the back of his hand tightened each time he lifted the mug. Then he set it down on the table and linked his fingers together, planting his chin on them as his lively dark eyes watched me. Big hands. Long fingers. I'd admired them a couple of days ago, too.

Maybe he plays the piano? Or the organ?

He's a vicar, Merry!

So?

"You're right about the parents," he said. "Her mother died around six months ago. Just on ninety. And her dad followed only weeks later. Don't ever tell me broken hearts don't exist." He looked down at his mug for a while and seemed to be having some sort of inner battle. His mouth twitched at the corners and he closed his eyes a couple of times as though he was seeing far-away things.

"I'm sure they do," I agreed. "But I've never had one. I married a man who valued me about as much as he did every other woman he took to bed. There was more relief than heartbreak when Duncan Skeene and I finally parted. Should have done it years earlier."

"Merry," Paul said with infinite tenderness, raising his gaze to mine again. "Pearls before swine. Jesus' words from The Sermon on the Mount. Did you get trampled, as Our Lord indicated the pearls would be if they were cast down in front of pigs?"

I swallowed, and shook my head. "I finally found the courage to trample him back. Hired a good lawyer and took him for half his worldly goods. He hated that. And he hated it even more when my parents died a few months later and Graham and I inherited their house. He missed out on a share of it."

Paul let out a brief chuckle. "Did your brother act for you?"

I know my eyebrows must have shot halfway up my forehead at his rather personal question. "No – a friend he recommended. It seemed a good idea to keep things further from home."

He unclasped his fingers and picked up his mug again. "Yes, families can sometimes be less than helpful. Not that I'm casting any aspersions on your brother." He took a sip of tea. "Margaret was certainly not much help to Isobel."

That made me wonder about *his* family, of course. Hadn't they wanted him to go into the Church? Or the Army? Or didn't you have to be in both to end up places like Afghanistan? I decided to enquire later instead of spoiling the easy conversation between us right now.

"What are you planning to do for dinner?" I asked. "There are plenty of eggs. And I saw pretty good-looking lettuces and herbs in the vegie garden. Omelet and salad? Quiche and salad? I have to eat, so you may as well too. Unless you've made other arrangements of course?"

It wasn't a very gracious invitation but I swear his big brown eyes lit up as though someone had thrown a switch. Maybe the way to a man's heart really is through his stomach, although that had never worked with my unlamented ex-husband.

"I won't outstay my welcome," Paul assured me. "Things to do later, but I haven't had a decent omelet in ages. Shall I go out and cut a lettuce?"

I was pleased he'd chosen omelets because quiche would have been a fiddle. "Yes, if you don't mind." I rattled around in the knife drawer and handed him a sharp wooden-handled number, then peered into the fridge and pantry, wondering what I could use for filling. "There's cheese," I said. "Tinned mushrooms? Baked beans?"

He rose from his chair. "Merry, anything will be a treat for a man who lives primarily on frozen dinners. I haven't had mushrooms for a while?" That sounded like a definite suggestion to me, even couched as a careful question, so I pulled out the can of mushrooms.

"But you get enough baked beans?"

He shrugged. "They make an easy lunch."

Yes, they do. I eat my share when I'm working on manuscripts at home in my study.

While he was outside I started warming the mushrooms in the microwave oven, set a small heavy frying pan on the stove to heat, and got the gas going again. By the time he came back I'd beaten the eggs in two small bowls (three for him, two in the other for me), added salt and pepper and a dash of milk to each, and was about to slice some tomatoes into wedges for the salad.

Rather to my surprise Paul put the lettuce into the sink

and proceeded to strip off the outer leaves and tear up the middle, so I grabbed a couple of dinner plates and some cutlery.

"You're domesticated after all," I said.

"Not a total loss in that department." His lips quirked but his attention didn't leave the lettuce.

Hmmm. Secretive. I took a chance and asked, "Presumably you're not married if you're here eating with me?"

"No, Merry. I'm not fit husband material right now." He said it in a flat voice which gave little away, but it had a definite tone of 'back off'.

Okay... I can take a hint.

"The dogs and I spent the morning at the Burkeville café," I said, wondering if I'd get a reaction to that.

Well, yes, I did, but not one that got me any further. "They run a good business there. Great pizzas. You saw their wood-fired oven?" He pushed the outer lettuce leaves to one end of the sink.

I shook my head. "Sounds good for next time though. John was on the beach here yesterday."

That *certainly* pushed his buttons. "Here?" he demanded. "Right along here at The Point?"

"Surfing," I said, sliding the wedges of tomato from the chopping board into a glass bowl I'd found. "No wetsuit. He must be impervious to the cold. He came up through the garden. Scared me witless for a moment."

"Are you okay?"

Hmmm, fast reply, full of concern. Good.

"Yes, of course I am. He made me a cup of tea."

"You let him into the house when you were alone?"

Excellent reaction! Brows drawn together, vertical wrinkle between them, a fierce sniff and a backward tilt of his head. Absolutely seething, although I wasn't sure why I was enjoying winding him up so much.

"I let *you* in, didn't I?" Let him think on that. But after a couple of seconds I took pity on him and added, "I think finding Isobel had just properly sunk in. I was shaky. May have even gone weepy on him, and he went into macho protective mode when he saw the fingerprint powder on the door. Did you find the parsley?"

Paul closed his eyes for a couple of seconds. I could easily imagine he was mad at himself for forgetting it because he turned away without speaking and returned with a handful of parsley plus some spears of chives and a stem of new mint. I don't usually put mint in salads. "Do you like this?" I asked, crushing it to release the scent and waving it under his nose.

He sniffed and recoiled. "Maybe with roast lamb. I just grabbed whatever I could see that looked herby. It's definitely getting darker out there."

"Probably be a spectacular sunset, then," I said, tossing the mint aside. "I love it when the clouds get lit up by the low sun and change color." I pushed the chopping board across to him. "Shred the herbs up and throw them in with the lettuce and tomatoes. And give it a shake of this." I'd found a bottle of vinaigrette dressing in the fridge while I was fossicking.

Turning my attention to the pan, I dropped a knob of butter-substitute onto the hot surface. It sizzled fiercely and melted very fast so I tipped the bowl of three seasoned eggs in and began to draw the cooked portions aside, tilting the pan this way and that so the raw remainder ran underneath. "Sit," I said, and Paul did.

In another thirty seconds I ladled a portion of warmed mushrooms onto it and curled it onto his plate. Very professional, even if I do say so myself. The surface that had been underneath was now on top, gleaming golden and looking like a crumpled quilt.

Another sizzle as the other bowl of eggs hit the pan.

"Start without me," I said, but he didn't. From the corner of my eye I saw him bow his head and whisper what I assumed was grace. Sixty seconds later I set my own omelet on the table and then Paul picked up his fork. "Very slick," he said. "You've done that before." He took a mouthful and groaned his appreciation. Yes, it was good. We sat happily scoffing, ignoring the dogs who thought they deserved some too.

Once we'd made a good start I asked him if Bruce Carver had called on him. "He was here bright and early this morning," I added.

Paul's good humor disappeared in an instant. "What a slippery weasel. I felt guilty. Me, who checked if she was okay and would have revived her if it had been possible. He as good as accused me of being a criminal."

"I didn't like him either," I agreed. "But it must be a

horrible job. Having to be suspicious of everyone he comes across in his working day – apart from other policemen of course."

He quirked an eyebrow. "You're too generous, Merry."

"Detective Wick was nicer. Nicer in manner, I mean."

Paul forked up some more omelet. "I doubt I told them anything they hadn't already heard from the uniformed constables or the paramedics."

"Or Margaret, or me. Did anyone find the murder weapon?"

"In the church?" His eyes widened. "Not as far as I know. They took away the shards of the broken vase in case it was that. It wouldn't have been a gun or a knife. Unless it was very large and they'd used it as a club."

"Euw," I said. "Best not to think about it. And why wouldn't they just shoot her or stab her, if so?"

"Best not to think about that, either," Paul replied, turning away and avoiding my gaze while he concentrated very hard on getting some salad to stay on his fork.

There was a sudden patter of rain on the window glass. "You should have parked closer," I said.

He shook his head. "Won't hurt me to run for it. It's not far. And it mightn't last long. These sudden little showers often just buzz off out to sea."

I stood and switched on the light. It was getting darker by the second. I gasped as I peered out the window. "Lightning. We're in for a –"

My comment was drowned by an enormous boom of

thunder that shook the whole house. Dramatic enough that I couldn't believe it would stay on its foundations. I hate thunder and was glad I had company, but Paul gave an inhuman howl, dropped his knife and fork so they crashed onto the table, and then the floor, and wrapped his arms around his head.

I was astounded a big man like him would react like that. All I could do was stare, open-mouthed, as the thunder rolled on and on, making the house tremble and rumble. He stayed frozen, eyes tightly closed from what I could see through his fingers.

After several seconds I staggered to my feet, accidentally kicked one of the teddies who'd bolted out of the dog bed at the noise, and managed to get an arm around Paul's shoulders. The poor man was shaking and shuddering, and both dogs were howling hideously.

It's not often I'm the most cool-headed presence in the room but this time I won hands-down. Paul tried to shake me off but I wasn't budging. He was silent and panting now. I really think he would have dived under the table with the dogs if there'd been room.

His reaction to Isobel's body and the possibility of an intruder in the church rushed back to me. Afghanistan. Gunfire and death. Hideous wounds and blood.

All too slowly the thunder died away, gradually losing volume as it rolled out over the sea. Then the rain started pelting in earnest, splashing through the open window and bouncing up off the counter. I slid my arm away from his shoulders and dragged on the catch to slam it closed, pleased with the excuse to turn aside because I knew Paul would hate me seeing him like this. The noise of the drumming rain receded as a result, and one of the teddies took the opportunity to scuttle out to the knife and fork and lick up some eggy remnants from the floor. It was enough to bring a little relief.

"Stop that, Greedy-guts," I said, bending to retrieve the utensils. I put them in the sink, careful to do it quietly. Then I chose clean ones from the drawer, placing them on the table beside Paul so he could continue eating if he regained his appetite. I went to wipe up the mess on the floor and found a small pink tongue had already done the job for me.

Paul took his time to sit up straight. He took a lot longer to look me in the eye. "So now you know why I'm in the 'peaceful' colonies," he finally said, bitterness twisting his lips.

"PTSD," I said – a statement rather than a question.

He nodded. "The Church found me a quiet location where I'm supposed to be recovering from the nightmares and flashbacks and general anxiety the war trauma caused."

"There'll be more thunder yet," I warned. "But at least you'll know it'll be thunder next time." Right on cue there was another huge boom, and although he flinched it was a less extreme reaction.

"Yes, it helps to know," he agreed, flexing his hands into fists and relaxing them again several times in a row as though it was something he did to calm himself.

"So it would have been terrible for you, finding Isobel like that."

State the obvious – why don't you, Merry.

He blew out a big gusty breath. "Especially in my church, which is my sanctuary. My place of peace." He swallowed a couple of times, his throat working visibly. "The hell of it was," he added quietly, "I was supposed to be there to give comfort to the troops. To those who were hurt and anxious themselves. I saw too many of them badly wounded, close to death, dying in front of my eyes..."

I lowered myself onto the chair opposite him again. "It would take a very strong person to cope with that," I confirmed. Another flash of lightning brightened the room for an instant. We both waited, still and tense, for the accompanying boom of thunder, and I quietly counted out loud. It took five seconds to start. The storm was moving away. "It's going," I said. "Come into the sitting room for a few minutes. I'll draw all the curtains in there and put some music on. Hide the weather, and drown it out with something soothing." I reached for his hand.

He was slow to rise from the chair but allowed me to guide him through to the other room. I pulled the old linen curtains across the two windows to block out the possibility of seeing any more, and switched on the ancient radiogram. The Concert program sprang to life – as good as anything else I was likely to find. It sounded like one of Bach's Brandenburg Concertos, although I couldn't tell you which one. I lowered the volume and coaxed Paul to sit on the sofa. He rested his elbows on his knees and buried his forehead in his hands. I sat beside him and began to rub slow, soothing circles on his back, although it was hard not to speed up with that lively music. "There's sweet sherry if that would help relax you?" I suggested.

He pressed his lips together, plainly amused at such a useless suggestion. "Sweet sherry isn't the answer to the problem, Merry," he muttered. "Or to many problems at all. Alcohol of any kind is a bad idea for this."

"If we go forward in a logical manner, it might help?" I hazarded, still circling my palm on his back. "Not that I know much about it. Just being sensible. Can you eat any more? If you finish the rest of your omelet there's ice-cream."

He looked sideways at me as though I was treating him like a small boy. Perhaps I was. I'd never been in a situation like this. Never seen anyone so devastated.

"Rather lost my appetite for now – sorry. Just give me a few minutes, eh?"

We sat together without speaking further. The concerto's last notes ebbed away and the announcer said, "That was The New Zealand Chamber Orchestra." Another flash of lightning through the fawn linen curtains. Another roll of thunder. We both listened but even though it still sounded like booming gunfire, Paul had himself under iron control again.

He heaved a deep sigh, then straightened and glanced across at me. Pale. Embarrassed. But looking more together now. "That was an excellent omelet, Merry, but I think I'm done. See if the dogs want the last of it. There won't be much left."

I rose and walked quietly to the kitchen as something new started up on the old radio. Yes, we'd both almost finished but there was enough to give Itsy and Fluffy a morsel each. The moment I touched their bowls they scampered out from the dog bed again, encouraging me with grunts and wags before they fell to eating what I scraped off our plates.

Paul seemed to be recovering okay in the sitting room so I rejoined him. Rubbing his back any more felt out of the question so we listened to the music, and sometimes the receding thunder, until it had rolled right away.

"Ice-cream time," I said, rising from the sofa and indicating he should come back to the table. I'd seen a tub in the freezer. It may have been in there a little too long, but I peeled and chopped up a banana and a couple of fuzzy green kiwis from the fruit bowl to go with it and it was fine. No one was going to die from it anyway.

Something was bugging me though. I set the plates on the table and sat down opposite him again. "Paul, tell me to shut up if I'm crossing lines here. You have three churches to hold services in but they're not busy ones. Maybe you're getting too much time to think and worry?"

He picked up his fork and stabbed a piece of banana "Which is why I paint the fences and keep the gardens up to scratch. You New Zealanders are very self-sufficient. I'm not... needed... as much as I hoped to be."

I had a sudden memory of him tweaking a weed or two from one of the pots at the church as he walked out with PC Moody. "You're the gardener, too? The primulas and calendulas at St Agatha's are amazing this year. I thought as we were standing outside that it looked like flames and smoke." I decided to keep my 'rocket blasting off to heaven' description to myself. "You're not feeling useful enough, are you? That's no good for your spirits. Who do you think killed Isobel? Come on – good mental distraction," I added when he looked astounded.

"I'm not exactly DS Weasel."

I grinned at the name. "But you know people. You have different connections from mine. John at the Burkeville Bar?"

He shook his head. "I've no connection with him at all, apart from an occasional meal there. He'd have no reason to kill Isobel."

"And yet?" I said as suggestively as I could, "He wanted to buy her house out from under her."

Paul shook his head more firmly and then stopped. "Really?"

"He told me so himself, and said she wasn't willing to sell. He seemed annoyed."

"Not annoyed enough to kill her, surely?"

"No, I shouldn't think so," I conceded. "Do you know if Isobel owned the house outright? Might her parents have left it to both daughters, with a life interest for as long as Isobel needed to live there?"

"They might have. I don't know."

He scooped up some ice-cream and kiwi fruit, looking thoughtful, so I let him keep thinking.

"Given how much Margaret appeared to own compared to Isobel, that hardly seems fair though," he eventually said.

I grimaced. "Life's not always fair, but these things happen in families. You said the parents were almost ninety. People of that age don't think about changing their wills – if they even have one in the first place. Ask my brother... Margaret could have killed Isobel to hurry the process along."

His eyes really bugged out at that. "No Merry, I'm sure she didn't!" He shoveled some more ice-cream in as though he was using it as an excuse not to talk about something so distasteful.

"She wasn't far away from the church when it happened," I murmured. "Somewhere around the shops."

He began to cough, and I waited until he'd safely swallowed.

"Graham might know?" I suggested chasing a slice of banana around my plate to give him time to consider. "I'll ask him anyway. No harm done if he doesn't know."

"Or won't tell you." A hint of a grin followed that.

I relaxed a little more. This was going better between us now. "The rain's easing. I hope this old roof doesn't leak."

He cocked his head. "I don't hear anything overflowing. I'll check the gutters and downpipes for you before I go."

I nodded my thanks. "And *then*," I said, "We need to

consider Margaret's husband. I gather he wasn't the most scrupulous businessman."

"Tom Alsop?" Paul's eyebrows lifted. "What do you mean?"

"I've heard he's a very slow payer, among other things. Maybe because he needs money? Could he have bumped poor Isobel off? With a car jack, maybe? Something lethal and heavy like that from one of his car yards?"

Paul shook his head, as though indulging a child. "Have you ever touched a car jack, Merry?"

"No," I admitted. "Graham does all the car stuff. Or he gets Ten Ton Smedley to. There has to be some benefit in having a brother on hand."

Another faint grin. "I can think of much more suitable weapons. In fact a car yard would be *full* of better alternatives. So would the average garden shed. Anyway, following her into church where anyone else could turn up seems a very odd choice." He pointed at me across the table. "Why wouldn't he just come out here where it's isolated? Get her alone? Hit her with a big stone and leave her on the beach? Make it look as though she'd tripped over?"

"You're a bit too good at this," I said, and we returned to eating our dessert.

I held up a finger after a couple of minutes. "Okay, there's John's mate, Erik. We didn't consider him. He might have done something so John could get the house he wanted?"

"You're kidding me," Paul said, shaking his head. "I think John's plenty capable of doing his own dirty work."

"Why?"

"He was a navy SEAL, or something along those lines."

Huh! The body and the surf fell neatly into place.

"Erik's got an awful lot of teeth," I mused.

"Isobel wasn't gnawed to death..."

"No, but he's very smiley. As though he's hiding something."

Paul finished his last mouthful and set his spoon and fork down neatly in the center of his plate. "Give it a rest, Merry. Leave it to DS Weasel. Thank you for dinner – it was great."

"Or there's Lord Drizzle," I tried. "Wanting this piece of land back to add to his farm."

"So he can mine the uranium under it," Paul suggested with a totally straight face. After a few seconds he cracked up and slapped a hand on the table top.

I must have been looking so foolish – mouth gaping, eyes wide, actually believing...

"Anyway, I have someone for you," I said once I'd recovered from his uranium joke. "Rona Jarvis – old lady who could do with a few visits, and maybe some help. Lurline from the animal shelter rescued her cat and says she's arranged Meals on Wheels – for Rona, not the cat."

"Rona Jarvis... " Paul murmured. "Doesn't ring any bells."

"Could be before your time here. She might have been virtually house-bound for ages. A real recluse and invisible to the rest of the village." I stacked the empty dessert plates together. "What you don't see, you forget about easily enough. Check with Lurline."

Paul nodded, looking surprisingly keen to track Rona down. "Loneliness is very hard on some of the senior citizens. Sometimes just a friendly face and a few minutes of chat work wonders."

"Or a pretty cupcake from The Café," I agreed. "I could drop in with the odd goodie when I'm out for a walk."

"You could drop the odd goodie in to me, too," Paul surprised me by saying.

"Buy your own!"

He rolled his eyes. "That's the trouble – Iona won't let me pay. She seems to think I lead an impoverished life as a minister and can't afford treats."

"Do you need more treats, Paul?" I couldn't help asking.

I swear he blushed. He certainly couldn't look me in the eye any longer.

6

SPYING IN THE GARAGE

I MADE Paul a cup of hot sweet tea before we went outside again. They give that to people who donate blood, don't they? I was working on the theory that it might make him feel better.

He took his leave soon afterward, insisting on walking around the cottage first to make sure the guttering wasn't clogged up and water wasn't spilling over anywhere.

There were plenty of low bushes around but I guess the salty wind was enough to discourage many taller trees so there was no leaf build-up to worry about.

"How do you reckon she keeps all this so tidy?" I asked. "I mean it's not exactly house-and-garden, but it's a lot for one person. She has to have help of some kind, surely? With the lawns at least? I wonder who."

"Hardly lawns," Paul said, surveying the expanse of rather lumpy rough grass. He was probably picturing

English parks and cricket pitches. "But yes, it's been cut in the last couple of weeks or so. Be a devil of a job though."

I kicked at a hopeful dandelion flower which had shot up since the last mowing. "I could ask the man with the lawn service who does ours if he does these too."

Paul moved closer to the plot where he'd cut the lettuce. "She probably copes with the flowers and vegetables on her own. The over-all effect is good but it's weedy if you look closely."

"Needs your tender touch," I joked.

He bent to pat the teddies who were gamboling around with us, no doubt getting wet and muddy from the grass. I wondered whether I'd need to bath them, or at least give them a good brushing.

"Ironic, isn't it," he said as he straightened. "The first meal out I have in ages is on the same night I have an appointment with the school principal in Burkeville."

Lucy Stephenson. Heading for retirement, and so thin her wrinkles have wrinkles. Not competition.

I gave the dandelion another kick. "I've heard she's very well thought of. What are you planning?"

Paul took a deep breath of the salty air. It smelled different now, as though the lightning had changed it. "Activities for the older boys who don't have enough to do."

I privately hoped he didn't have Religious Studies in mind. "Such as?" I crossed my fingers behind my back.

"Basketball. Steven Adams has made it popular here, playing in Oklahoma so successfully, and some of those kids are already six-footers. I played at the base. It was a good way to get rid of... aggression."

I looked at him with real surprise. My mental picture of him bowing his head over a bible switched to a big hot man charging around as part of a team, hurling himself sideways to bump others out of the way. Dust and sweat and army sports gear. Grunts and curses and yells of triumph. No problem to imagine at all.

"So you're going to coach them?" I asked, trying to banish that image and confine him to a cassock and dog-collar again.

"Once the school has the hoops and backboards set up. Which will cost a bit, of course, but they have a fundraiser under way."

"Good for them," I said. "And good for you. I hope it goes well."

He glanced at his watch. "And keeps the kids off the streets. Speaking of going, I do need to be off. Lock the place up properly and... thanks for getting me through that."

"You got yourself through it, Paul," I said, attempting a smile. "I didn't have a clue what to do."

"You were there. It helped," he said, touching me on the arm before heading to the gate. "Sorry I've left you with the dishes."

"Pffft! Four plates, one salad bowl. I'm glad you were here. The dogs and I wouldn't have enjoyed the thunder much on our own."

And wasn't *that* the truth. I'd have been gibbering on the

floor if I'd been here alone when that first clap of thunder hit.

It took only five minutes to clean up. As I swished the dishes around in the sink I remembered what I'd been doing when Paul had unexpectedly arrived.

Snooping, basically.

It was still semi-light now the clouds had scudded away so I decided the garage was worth a quick check.

PC Henderson from Yorkshire said they'd found nothing amiss when the house was visited, but I presumed they'd been searching for blood and forced entry, not anything more personal yet. I'd hung the car keys and the garage door fob on a curly brass hook beside the fridge so I grabbed them, gave them a little toss from hand to hand, and muttered 'last chance' as I walked across the cracked and glistening wet concrete.

I was surprised there was something as modern as an electric garage door, but maybe the original timber one had rotted? Perhaps it would have cost more to replace it with a proper carpentry job than this ribbed metal? Or perhaps it was the original door after all because the garage was nowhere near as old as the house. I pressed the button, and the light flickered on as the door rolled up.

The little Mini crouched inside and there were full-height shelves against the wall at the far end. That was all. Shaking my head, I checked them out. Some old cans of paint, a packet of new windshield washer blades, a plastic container of engine oil with dribbles down it, short pieces of timber, dusty boxes. Just assorted rubbishy stuff any garage might have. The side window was draped with cobwebs. Defeated, I leaned on the nearest shelf and just about fell over.

It turned, smooth as silk, on some sort of mechanism. Behind the shelving was a small separate room. Lit by an overhead skylight. With a desk, a filing cabinet, and an iMac.

Bingo.

I held my breath. This was better than the exercise book of old household accounts! I'd bet a million bucks (if I had it) that the Police hadn't found it. It was invisible from the outside, with only the skylight in the flattish roof. It was invisible from the inside because the Mini looked as though it took up all the available space. Why would anyone presume otherwise? Who'd give more than a cursory glance?

So there *was* Wi-Fi and I wouldn't need to leave the old cottage to do my work. John had been convinced there wasn't, and I hadn't even thought to try turning my laptop on after his assertion. He'd said Isobel told him she had no computer. Which made me extremely curious about why she did. And why it was hidden like this.

I reached in and tapped a tentative finger on the Enter key. The screen immediately lit up.

WHAT? She'd gone out and left it turned on, presuming she'd be back soon, and it had simply gone to sleep in her absence? My lucky day – because if she'd hidden the computer like this it was a good bet her passwords would be well concealed, too.

Mindful I was really snooping now, I pressed the button on the fob. The garage door rolled down again, leaving me in humming silence and total privacy.

There was a desk lamp. I turned it on, knowing the light associated with the door would switch off in thirty seconds or so. And sure enough...

I checked out the swiveling shelves first. They swung easily on a solid-looking pivot I could just glimpse at the top and bottom now I knew something like that must exist. There was a push-in latch that hadn't been engaged. It was hidden behind a small cardboard box which held a few heavy old plumbing parts to anchor it in place, and there was just room for a little old lady's hand to slide behind to reach it. Isobel must have dashed out in a real hurry if she hadn't checked it was properly secured.

Once I could see there was no way I could trap myself, I pulled the swiveling shelves closed behind me so anyone trying to peer through the cobwebby side window would see nothing. Unlikely anyone was going to, but I was in full stealth mode now.

I sat. Expensive and comfortable chair. Maybe she'd spent a lot of time here? I didn't much like the feeling of being cut off from everything except the sky, but I guessed the place had been built for invisibility and it certainly worked on that level.

There were lots of ring-binders, meticulously labelled with the expected things like Accounts, House, Insurance, and Car. And unexpected things like Alsop A-One Autos, and Burkeville Bar. And totally unheard of things like Normie Hamilton and Soapworks. Soapworks? What?

There were several Smiggle notebooks with bright covers and designs of hearts and cats and flowers. The spines had a different year written on each.

I tapped on her email icon. Three unread messages – one from someone called Mario G, with *'New York accom'* in the subject line. One from a realtor, presumably with house listings. And one with no subject from Nam Cheng. A person or a company?

Would people know if I'd opened them? Plainly someone would eventually find the secret little den and could tell from the date that it hadn't been Isobel.

New York accom? I stared at that for a while because it made no sense. Finally my curiosity got the better of me.

Hi Isobel, I'm getting a list together for you and should be finished by tomorrow. Short term central city apartments with a separate bedroom are in short supply right now. Sure you wouldn't rather have a hotel for the duration?

Mario G, NYapartmentfinders.

The duration of what? My toes twitched, and my fingers fizzed, and my brain filled with fireworks. Surely she wasn't planning to leave the teddies behind?

I opened the realtor's next.

Good evening Ms Crombie. I've attached links to upmarket retirement facilities in Florida as you requested. Please let me know when you require further information about any of these.

Hannah Hertzog, Hertzog-Griffin Realtors Inc.

Upmarket retirement facilities? I doubted Isobel could afford anything upmarket in Drizzle Bay, let alone Florida. Who was she kidding? And why didn't she just do a search herself instead of asking someone else to? I clicked the first link. Marble columns – possibly faux. Fountains, gardens, card games, huge sociable lounges filled with wealthy-looking American people. Women with gnarled hands but curiously unlined faces below puffy blonde hairdos. Men with bristly moustaches and plaid sport jackets. The other links showed facilities just as extravagant, with palm trees, ocean views, golf courses. Isobel would have needed to upgrade her wardrobe if she had designs on places like these. And her face!

By now I had nothing to lose by opening Nam Cheng's as well.

Yes, ideal vehicles. Let me have address.

I planted both elbows on the desk and stared at the screen, willing the message to translate itself into something that made sense. Vehicles could be some sort of tie-up with Tom Alsop? I opened the doc folders and found Alsop A-One. Photographs. Nothing but a lot of very bad photographs. Maybe taken in a hurry so the subject wouldn't know? Each one was of an Asian person and most of them had a slice of Alsop A-One Autos showing in the back-ground. The file names were car registration plates. The slinky Indian gentleman with the gold chain at the open neck of his shirt... the chubby little chap who looked curi-ously like Kim Jong-un... the beautifully groomed Madam

Butterfly type... all had been labelled something like ABC 246. There were dozens of them. Next door to each was a photo of a luxurious car with an identical file name apart from one extra digit.

Before I knew it I'd gnawed the pink gel enamel off the end of my thumbnail. Isobel had been matching up wealthy people with expensive cars but there were no names or addresses. Nam Cheng wanted addresses. They had to be hidden here somewhere but I couldn't tell where without opening every file and folder.

I ground my teeth and chose the Burkeville Bar next. Would there be menus? Drinks lists? Was she a secret restaurant critic?

Soon the gel enamel was further off my thumbnail.

John Bonnington's 'father' was called Erik Jacobsen, so he must be a stepfather, and that'd be why he sounded different and looked nothing like John. And was probably younger than I'd assumed. It all made better sense now. But why on earth was Isobel keeping notes on them? Hopefully because they were one of the 'smaller businesses' she did the tax accounts for. Maybe she'd given the actual accounts a different file name?

For all I knew she was cooking up a plot for a thriller – one that no-one would ever read now. That had possibilities...

Perhaps she'd decided her 'characters' wanted to lie low for some reason. Well, they'd come to the ideal place. New Zealand is at the end of the world. It's so isolated that half the birds can't fly. And Drizzle Bay is small, with Burkeville only a little larger. Blips on the map. Somewhere to stop for a few minutes on the way north. A coffee and a slice of cheese-cake, a grin and a wave from the charming (and possibly gay) fellows who'd bought the place to escape the rat-race back in the States. Someone was chasing them. That's why they had those big German Shepherds. Yes, I could see a plot was possible there. A better one than the girl/boy/housekeeper manuscript I'd spent half the day wading through and correcting. And if John and Erik were gay I'd eat my hat. Or I'd eat Isobel's hat anyway, seeing I hadn't brought one with me. Those two men had testosterone squirting out of every pore.

I was so excited about my strange find that I really, really wanted someone to talk to. My skin felt tight and crawly. Shivers danced up and down my spine. This was the most fun I'd had in ages, and I didn't want my toys taken away.

I glanced at my watch. How would the time work? Not good. It was afternoon for my all-time best friend Steff because she now lives half the world away in Montreal. We'd met on our first day at school, and even with all those thousands of miles separating us these days we trust each other implicitly. If I sent Isobel's stuff into the cloud I'd still have access to it. For sure the Police would find it sooner or later but I wanted it as well. I could have a good look first, plead surprise and curiosity, and then tell Bruce Carver. I'm sure he'd be livid I'd found it first, though.

I decided to let Steff know about it, just as insurance. She wouldn't be implicated in the least if she didn't retrieve it. I hoped. But she'd be at work so I'd have to wait until morning, add six hours, and remember it was yesterday for her. I was too tired to calculate that. I'd try asking Graham about Isobel's house ownership instead. Surely he'd be back from Rotary by now?

I pushed the expensive chair away from the desk, and stood. Goodness, I was really achy after sitting for so long. I did a couple of shoulder rolls, pushed the hinged shelving aside, and peered out into the dark garage. The dim beam from the desk lamp showed nothing amiss but I tiptoed to the window all the same. It was eerily still outside after the earlier lashing rain and wind but really I could see diddly. I pushed the button on the door fob and the main light flashed on as the garage's metal door rolled up. I snapped off the desk lamp, secured the pivoting shelves, and ran for it, reversing the door so it closed once I was clear. It felt good to be safely inside the cottage again and even better to be climbing into bed with a cup of tea a few minutes later.

Time to see if brother dear was willing to talk. The phone rang and rang and I was about to hang up when he suddenly answered it, sounding harassed, and accompanied by a lot of barking.

"Merry? Can I call you back? I've just got in and the boys need feeding."

Sure Graham, dogs before sister...

"Fine," I said, rather abruptly. And cut him off.

But true to his word (he always is) he returned my call as

I was setting my empty cup on the top of the bedside chest, so good timing, bro.

"Graham," I began. "Are you eating okay on your own?" I thought it best to show some sisterly concern before bombarding him with the questions I really wanted answers to. "I can make you a curry or something tomorrow? I'll be calling in to collect a few more clothes."

"No Sis, all good," he said. "Can I put your name down for the December beach clean-up?"

"Ummm...?"

"Rotary's next project. If we get twenty or more people each willing to spare an hour or two we can comb through the main beach for litter and have it nicely cleaned up for Christmas visitors. With any luck, if they find the place clean, they'll leave it clean. And we're sponsoring two new garbage bins, too."

"Good for you," I said. "Yes, of course I'll help." After all, any excuse for a prowl on the beach on a nice day, and I could trade that for the info I was after. "Look, this cottage I'm minding. I'm wondering one little thing. Pure curiosity on my part. The old girl who owned it – Isobel Crombie – is she the sole owner or does she only have a life interest in it? I mean, might her sister automatically get it now? If the parents left it to them jointly?"

"Hmm..." he said.

To my secret pleasure I heard the clink of ice against the side of a crystal tumbler so he'd settled down with a drink which would probably help to loosen his tongue.

"As I recall...." he began. "Good boy, Manny – bring it here."

Even better! If he had the spaniels distracting him he might let more slip.

"Yes, as I recall, a life interest. The other sister got them organized."

"Margaret Alsop?"

"That's her. The parents, who'd had a will prepared by the firm when they'd been married only a year or so, had left everything to each other and then to their only daughter after they passed on. They'd let it slide for the ensuing sixty years and forgotten they'd never included the second girl." He clicked his tongue and I wondered if it was with disapproval for the lack of legal follow-up or to attract the spaniels.

"Wow," I said. "That's pretty bad. Good that Margaret realized it and got things organized because now her sister's dead I suppose it would have left a real legal tangle?"

"Well, not good, not good," Graham conceded.

"You don't think it's suspicious she got things in order and then Isobel died?" I asked in my best casual voice.

"Merry! Good heavens!" Yes, Graham was as shocked as I expected.

"It's only," I added quickly, "that someone I know is interested in buying the place and is wondering who will own it now."

Graham coughed, possibly still considering my thinly veiled suggestion that Margaret might have anything to do with her sister's death. "It'll take a while for probate to be confirmed," he said. "A few weeks for sure."

"She hardly needs the money," I murmured. "They have a lovely house, and they're currently away on a cruise. Anyway, thanks for that. It was all I wanted to know."

Sisterly cunning is a wonderful thing. If Graham doesn't think I want anything else then he prolongs the conversation with things he finds interesting. And this evening it was the possibility of Margaret killing Isobel. Yes!

"Sororicide," Graham said. "That's the legal term for killing a sister."

I looked sideways at my empty cup, annoyed I'd finished the tea. If Graham was in the mood to talk then I was in the mood to listen. "I'm sure she didn't. It'll just be a coincidence." And then I couldn't resist. "How long ago did the parents change the will?"

"Not long before they died. The two Alsops came in, each holding the elbow of one of the parents. I had to get Jenny to wheel in some extra chairs. They didn't look as though they'd make it as far as the boardroom."

Bingo! "Tom was there too? What business was it of his?" I demanded. "And you weren't suspicious? You didn't think to ask Isobel if it was okay with her?"

Graham cleared his throat – always his default when he's playing for time. "It was no business of hers. It was the parents who'd made the original will, and they wanted to correct an oversight – a situation caused by the passage of time."

"And the main new beneficiary made sure they got it done." Now it was my turn to clear my throat. "Did they seem of sound mind? That seems fishy to me, Graham. In fact lots of things are sounding fishy to me." He tried interrupting but I barreled ahead. "The moment people knew I'd been with the vicar when Isobel was found dead they started asking things and coming up with theories as to why she was killed. For instance, did she learn secrets from the tax returns she prepared for the local businesses?"

"Well... er..."

"Because someone bothered to track her down at the church and do the dirty. She knew a lot about what went on in Drizzle Bay, even though she looked so meek and mild."

I heard the slight rattle of the tags on one of the spaniels' collars. Maybe Graham was patting either Manny or Dan while he thought about that.

"She'd have known the state of their finances," he conceded. "Their taxable assets. Exemptions. How to minimize the amount they'd owe. But not much more."

"What about money laundering? Foreign currency transfers? Hiding money overseas?"

"You're into the realms of fantasy now, Merry," he snapped. "You've been editing too many thrillers."

"It's not *me* coming up with these theories," I pointed out. "I'll be really interested to hear what the Police discover eventually. I guess they'll find her files (I crossed my fingers) and have a good look at them. Maybe they'll find 'irregularities'. Just saying..."

"And hell might freeze over first," Graham shot back. "I think you're hoping for scandal where none exists. She was an unremarkable and law-abiding woman who lived a normal, straightforward life."

"And yet," I said, with more glee that I should have. "Someone killed her. They didn't do that for no reason at all. You don't creep up behind an old lady arranging the church flowers and mistake her for a master criminal. There must have been something going on below the surface."

"Good chap, good chap," I heard Graham mutter as the collar tags rattled again. Then he took an audible breath. "I'll keep my ears open, but don't expect anything at all. I think you're imagining problems and creating drama with no foundation. What time are you calling by tomorrow? The boys will be pleased to see you."

"I might bring the teddies again," I said, recognizing my cue to change the subject. "They'll all enjoy another run around together." I wriggled my shoulders deeper into the pillows. "I'll probably be there early afternoon. Sure you don't want that curry? I thought I'd make a double dose and bring some back here. This kitchen's nowhere near as nice as ours."

"Ah. Well, if it's not too much trouble," he agreed. "Sleep well, Merry."

"You too, Graham."

I was restless. My brain didn't want to turn off. Should I get up and make another cup of tea? Or get a glass of water? I lay there listening to the steady wash of the waves and surprised myself by missing Graham's quiet but steady presence. It wasn't long before I heard the patter of little doggie paws and a pair of enquiring white faces with black eyes peeked around the door. Company! I snapped my fingers and they scrambled up, settling either side of my feet. That felt a whole lot better. I switched off the bedside lamp and kept thinking.

7

LORD DRIZZLE OF DRIZZLE BAY

THE FOLLOWING morning I locked the old cottage up securely, made sure I had the blue lead on Fluffy and the pink one on Itsy, and set off for a good walk to kill some time. We progressed up Drizzle Bay Road as far as Drizzle Farm and found Lord Drizzle himself inspecting the pile of logs left over from the tree shredding I'd heard and seen yesterday. The same lanky boy in the precariously suspended jeans was mooching around, retrieving occasional lengths of timber and stacking them on one side.

"Morning Uncle Jim!" I called as I drew closer. I wouldn't call him that in public, but my father and Jim Drizzle had been good friends and he'd liked me calling him 'uncle' when I'd been younger.

"Little Merry," he said warmly. "What are you doing passing by on this lovely day? Been to see Lisa?" He eyed the teddies as though that proved the point.

I stopped, pleased he seemed in the mood to chat. "No, not taking these two to the vet. I'm house-and-pet sitting at poor Isobel Crombie's place. Arranged in rather a hurry by her sister."

"Shocking thing to happen. Shocking," Jim said, tugging his shapeless old stockman's hat off and clasping it over his heart as though he was at a memorial service. His very hairy silver eyebrows shone impressively in the sunlight. The boy in jeans rather spoiled the moment by throwing another piece of tree down on the pile and starting a mini landslide of rolling logs.

"Careful, Alex," Jim admonished. "Watch your toes."

As the helper was clumping about in orange forestry gumboots I doubted his toes were in much danger because they'd be steel-capped and chainsaw proof. He glared at Jim Drizzle from under beetling black brows and began to re-stack the timber. He didn't look at me at all.

"Who do you think did it?" I asked Jim. I've always been one for asking direct questions because you sometimes get surprising answers.

"Beats me," he said, cramming his hat back on. "Pleasant little woman. Nice mother too. Old Crombie was a hell of a drinker, but the brother-in-law stepped in and did what he could."

Huh? Was someone actually sticking up for Tom Alsop?

"Tom Alsop?" I asked, wanting to be certain that was who he meant.

The boy looked across again, wide-eyed this time. Something had grabbed his attention for sure.

"That's him," Jim said. "Generous chap. He built them a garage to keep the Mini in. The salt spray would have rusted it out otherwise."

"Didn't they have money for their own garage?" Suddenly the lack of alcohol made sense. Not many houses would have half a bottle of sweet sherry as their entire supply. Maybe that had been Isobel's private treat after her old soak of a dad had died?

"I fear they didn't," Jim said. "It all went down old Crombie's throat. But Tom Alsop's a car man, and there was no point letting a car sit out in this corrosive air."

He raised his face and sniffed the briny breeze like a dog. I saw there was hair up his nose about as bushy as his eyebrows and looked away in a hurry.

"So he arranged to get a garage built for them, and he paid for it, too," he continued.

"How long ago?" It was none of my business, but Jim seemed in a chatty mood. "It looks a bit dilapidated now."

"Salt spray and onshore winds," he said. "You can imagine what they would have done to that little car. Must have been about fifteen years ago. What year's the car?"

I shrugged.

"Not that that'll tell you much. It was bought second-hand of course." He looked down to where the teddies were enthusiastically sniffing at his boots. "You enjoying yourselves there, fellas?" he asked, bending down to pat them.

"Are you smelling sheep or cattle or my dogs in that mud?" He laughed as though it was an oft-repeated joke. Whatever they were finding it had their tails waving like feathery metronomes.

"The Police dropped the car back and put it in the garage so I haven't needed to go in there," I said.

Why was I lying? And what would it matter anyway?

Jim scratched his chin. "Pretty basic, I imagine. Just a bit of shelter for the car, but he kept an eye on the quality of the construction for sure. Tom's not short of a penny, but he wanted his money's worth." He glanced over his shoulder. The boy was now scrolling through his phone, apparently oblivious to anything else. Jim raised his eyebrows at me. "What *do* they find to get lost in all the time? My granddaughters are just as bad."

Jim hadn't seen it, but I had. The boy had shot a fast glance in our direction and then looked down at the screen again. He was definitely listening. That was twice he'd been interested in Tom Alsop. Something else to wonder about.

"Mustn't hold you up," I said, trying to encourage the dogs away from his boots. "I'll feel better once I hear they've arrested someone for Isobel's murder."

"Isolated place for a woman to live alone."

"Well, yes, but she seemed perfectly safe there. Who'd have expected her to die in the church with people only yards away?"

We both shook our heads, and then I thought to ask about the lawn-mowing service. Maybe they worked for Jim, too? "I want to find out who mowed Isobel's grass because it needs doing again soon. And if I'm in charge this week...?" I let the suggestion hang in the air.

"No idea, Merry. Harry Benson from Greenaway does ours here."

"Ours too. I'll give him a call. Bye for now." I gave the leads another twitch. "Come on, you two." Most reluctantly the little dogs deserted the Drizzle boots and we went on our way, keeping well to the side of the road in case vehicles came by. None did. Drizzle Farm and Isobel's cottage were the last pieces of civilization along here.

So Tom Alsop had overseen the garage. Did that mean the hidden office was his, built to his specifications? Somewhere to keep secret things separate from his work premises? Or had it always been an office for Isobel? And if it was, why had it been hidden like that? Or had she found it by accident and demanded a share in whatever he was doing there in return for her silence? My head was spinning with possibilities.

The phone was ringing when I returned. It threw me into a panic because although I could hear it, I had no idea where to find it. I followed the noise to an ancient cream landline model half hidden behind a curtain on the wall of the central hallway. It was still ringing imperiously even though I'd taken a while to get there. I lifted the heavy receiver with its tangled spiral cord. "Hello?"

"Yeah. It's me. Alex. About the grass."

It took me a few minutes to compute that. Grass? Marijuana?

"From this morning," he added. "At Jim's."

Isobel's lawns! Well, if not quite lawns, then certainly grass.

"Forty bucks to mow it," he added.

Ah – he was after pocket money. Forty dollars seemed reasonable for the amount of work involved. Had he any idea how much land there was? I wouldn't do it for forty, but I wasn't an underpaid (or unpaid) teenager, desperate for cash.

"Are you related to Jim?" I asked. I hadn't expected that, although now I thought back Jim had seemed kindly towards him and worried he might hurt himself with the logs.

"No."

"Oh. To Isobel? I'm so sorry you've lost her."

"No." Growled with impatience and something approaching anger. I decided to be quiet.

"I'm Tom Alsop's son. He never wanted to know me, but I've come to find him and get some justice for my mother."

Well, strike me down with a feather! So Tom had been playing away. "How old are you?" I demanded.

"Sixteen."

Tom must be over sixty, so it would have been a mid-life-crisis affair. Maybe he hadn't been married to Margaret back then? Another darn thing I needed to discover.

I sat down on the carved camphorwood chest in the hall-way, feeling the edges of the Chinese dragons and pagodas and trees biting into my bottom, and hoping it would hold my weight. "When did your mother know him?"

"Durr. Seventeen years ago." I practically saw his eyes roll.

"And you're sure about this? That you're his son?"

"It's what Mum finally told me, so I want to meet him."

Understandable. I changed ears with the phone. "You're going to have to wait a few more days. He's off on a cruise right now with his wife."

A short silence. Then a word which I won't repeat here. "So when's he back?"

Ignore the language, Merry, I told myself. *He's only a kid.*

"About a week. I'm looking after things for a while. Until they're home and someone decides what's happening with the cottage and the dogs."

"Bummer. So can I do the lawns?"

"Yes. Sometime in the next few days? I'll have to check and see if there's a mower, though. She might have used a regular lawn-mowing service."

Alex snickered. "Nope. There's a mower. I called in a couple of mornings back and asked if she had any jobs that needed doing. She tore out of the garage and showed me."

I shivered as though someone had just walked over my grave. "You must have been almost the last person to see her alive."

He sniffed. "I guess. I heard she died. That's why I thought I'd better ask again. She said forty bucks. So do you want the lawns mowed?"

"Fair enough," I said, trying hard not to sound spooked. Poor Isobel had probably been ready to leave for her fateful trip to the church.

And now I had the answer to why she hadn't locked the secret office behind her. She'd dashed out expecting heaven knows who, pulled the shelves closed but not locked them, and then forgotten to after being held up for a while by Alex.

"Who mowed the grass before this?"

I heard him sigh at the inquisition. "One of the farm helpers. German guy, here for work experience."

"Jim Drizzle didn't seem to know about that this morning when I asked."

Half a scornful laugh. "Jim doesn't know everything. He doesn't know who my father is, for starters."

There was a sudden storm of barking from the kitchen and the flip of the dog door. It sounded like someone was outside.

"Okay Alex – need to go. The dogs are upset about something. Thanks for offering." I hung the old receiver up after a fight with the curly cord and hurried through to the kitchen. There was no-one there, but the teddies led me out to the mailbox, prancing and yipping and urging me to follow them. I lifted the lid of the box and a large plastic courier envelope unfolded itself, shining in the sun and threatening to sail off in the salty breeze. What the heck? I hadn't heard anyone arriving, although maybe over Alex's voice and the dogs' noisy greeting, that wasn't entirely surprising. There was no vehicle when I looked along Drizzle Beach Road so it must have turned up past the farm and taken the shorter route back to the village. No surprise there.

"Shush!" I hissed at the teddies. There wasn't much of an improvement but perhaps I heard the engine of one of those DX motorcycle couriers receding into the distance?

I reached for the envelope, which sprang flatter once I grabbed it out of the box. Addressed to Tom Alsop. Who was sending stuff to him here? And what was on all those pages inside it?

Have you ever tried to get one of those self-stick plastic envelopes open? Not a hope unless you totally wreck it. I poked about under the flap with one finger, tried to peer inside, and admitted defeat. But if he had mail arriving here that strengthened my suspicions the office was probably still something to do with him. 'Curiouser and curiouser' – to quote an author a lot more famous than any of those I get to edit.

There was no way I could keep this secret from DS Carver and Detective Wick, but I could probably delay it until tomorrow. I might have been out all afternoon and not found it until I returned in the evening, mightn't I?

And that reminded me to check the time, because Stephanie in Montreal should be home from the patisserie by now. I sent her a teasing text, and to my surprise and plea-sure she texted back almost straight away.

Stephanie: *Secret files? Are you drunk?*
Merry: *Sober as. It's barely midday. So I've got you interested?*
Stephanie: *With a line like that? You bet.*

Merry: Are you free to FaceTime?

Stephanie: Yes, in five minutes because I'm going out for dinner soon. Need a cuppa.

Brilliant! By the time Steff had her tea, my laptop was open, ready and waiting. She looked all lit up and even more gorgeous than usual.

"Are you going out somewhere special?" I asked. "Or rather, *with* someone special?"

"Early days yet," she said. "If I expect nothing, I won't be disappointed."

"Expect *everything*," I said. "You just might get it. You deserve it. I bet it's cold?" It was close to summer in Drizzle Bay, so winter in Montreal.

"Hovering around minus twenty," she said. I watched as she pulled a blanket around her shoulders. She was wearing quite a skimpy dress.

I shuddered.

"Lots of early snow this year," she added, seeing my reaction. "A huge chunk of the city budget goes into snow removal. There are constantly graders and other machines pushing it about." She took a sip of her tea. "So," she said. "Secret files. This better be good."

"It might be very bad instead." I knew that'd get her even more interested. "Anyway," I added before she could interrupt, "There was an elderly lady murdered in the church here. The vicar and I found her." I waited for the expected exclamations this time.

"Murdered? Oh, Merry – how awful for you."

"Yes, grim doesn't begin to describe it," I agreed.

"But hang on… You? In a church? With a vicar?"

And there was the Steff I knew and loved. Even after a long day's work she was quick-witted and curious.

"Yes," I said, wishing I'd thought to make tea as well. "Remember I said I might try house minding? I was putting a notice on the community board and got chatting with him. He looked nothing like a vicar at this stage because he was painting the church fence in shorts and a T-shirt."

"O-kayyyyyy." she said. "But murdered? How?"

I heaved a big sigh. "Yes, it was totally horrible. The vicar realized his church flower-arranging lady had been inside for a long time so we went in to make sure she was all right. And she wasn't. She was dead on the floor, and bleeding from a head wound."

"Yikes!" Steff exclaimed. "Sorry – this is taking a while to sink in. And you saw her?"

"'Fraid so. Nasty. Apart from Mum and Dad after the accident I've never seen anyone dead." I squeezed my eyes closed remembering the awful night Graham and I had identified them, his quaking arm around my equally quaking shoulders.

"Don't, Merry. Try not to remember them like that."

I opened my eyes again and sent her a weak smile. She'd known them well. It had been practically as bad for her as losing her own parents.

"Anyway, we called the emergency services, cops and ambulance came, sister of the old lady was across the road shopping. The upshot was two dogs who needed looking after in a seaside cottage for a week, and that's what I'm doing."

"The dead lady's dogs? I thought I didn't recognize that wallpaper in the background."

I glanced behind me to the faded garlands of roses on the wall. "Yes, wouldn't be my choice. It might be older than me."

She grinned. "Bet Graham would like it."

"Really?" I said, rolling my eyes.

Her grin became a giggle. "Gotcha!"

"The murdered lady told someone I know that she didn't have a computer, which was a bind for me because I need Wi-Fi for my work. But I've found one very well hidden away and still running. I'm sure the Police don't know about it yet so I thought I'd have a look."

Steff took a slow sip of her tea and looked at me very directly with her dark brown eyes. "Be careful Merry. You might be getting into something nasty if she's been murdered."

"No 'might' about it. I'm sure I am. But I'm also hooked on it because some of this stuff is fascinating."

I knew she needed to finish getting ready to go out so I hurried things up. She had to be planning on wearing more than that dress if it was so cold outside. "Look – I just wanted someone else to know about the files. I think I'll send them to my Dropbox account because I'd be interested to have another dig through them." I took a deep breath. "It's odd she was murdered because she was such a sweet old thing.

Harmless, dowdy, poor as a church mouse. The sort of person you wouldn't look twice at."

Steff nodded, eyebrows raised, waiting for more.

"Except maybe she wasn't. The files are weird... and seeing I'm here with time on my hands.... what harm will it do if I dig around in them and see what I can come up with? No-one will know."

"You could just transfer them to a thumb-drive," she said.

"But that would be *stealing*, Steff. An actual physical thing, not just files floating around heaven knows where."

My brain surely does work in strange ways – it was stealing either way, and I knew that perfectly well.

I prodded a finger at her image. "And wouldn't a transfer like that lead them directly to me? To be honest I don't have a clue, but I told you I was on a jury a few months earlier? The Police computer forensics man was fascinating. He could tell *everything* that had been going on. He had the whole chain of messages where the accused made contacts on the Dark Web and tried to buy illegal substances. All the fake names they used, and where they got the money from and moved it to."

"Beyond me to know," she said, shaking her head and then upending the last of her cup of tea. "I'm a baker, not a nerd." She set the cup down and gave a luxurious stretch and a yawn. "I'm finally winding down from work and can probably be good company now, but you be careful."

"Good luck with Francois," I said, straight-faced.

"Lucien," she corrected. "Oops!"

"Lucien," I repeated, glad to at least get his name out of

her. "And of course I'll be careful. Have fun." I gave her a little wave before she disappeared from the screen.

I had no idea what I thought Steff could do from half the world away, except... if anything odd happened to me, at least she could let someone know the files existed – floating around in 'the cloud' once I'd done it – wherever that actually is.

Tell the cops tomorrow, Merry.

Maybe.

No maybe about it! You're allowed another half day and then DS Weasel has to know.

Maybe.

It truly was a delicious puzzle; I knew I'd be worrying at it all the rest of the day.

Why were the car people foreign? Were John and Eric really father and son? What was in that courier envelope addressed to Tom? Why had he built the secret office? (I was becoming ever more certain he'd been using it, because if Isobel had needed an office she could have used a spare bedroom, surely?)

Why was Isobel interested in US real estate? Or was it Tom? How had Alex tracked Tom here? And what would become of the teddies once I'd done my week in the cottage?

The biggest questions of all remained; who murdered Isobel – and why?

8

A VISIT FROM SURFER JOHN

I WAS WISHING NOW that I'd asked Alex for his cell number. I could hardly phone Jim Drizzle and ask him to give Alex a message from me without making His Lordship suspicious. However, the teddies were always on for a walk so I decided to have lunch, follow that up with another look at the files, and then take the road past Drizzle Farm again – me hoping for a glimpse of Jim or Alex, and the teddies no doubt looking forward to another whiff of stinky boots.

There was most of a bag of sliced bread in the freezer and cheese in the fridge. Surprisingly good cheese. Blue from Kapiti and Vintage cheddar from Mainland. I ate some chunks of the lovely blue while I waited for two slices of bread to toast under the grill. Then I flipped them over and layered some Vintage on the other side, peppered it well, and slid it back until the cheese had melted and was hot and runny and delicious. A glass of wine would have made it a perfect lunch but no wine in sight, sadly.

I added some to my mental shopping list. Steak for the curry, wine for whenever, something to make a change from the Pup-E-Love for the teddies, real butter (because Isobel only had a pot of something pale yellow, ambitiously labelled 'spread'), and I'd better check she had decent rice in the pantry, too.

The teddies were snoozing in the dotty dog bed so I tiptoed out with my laptop and locked the house. That may have been overkill, but if I was going to be concealed in the secret office then anyone could sneak into the house. A surfer, a vicar, a motorbike courier...

I signalled the garage door to open. The teddies heard it rolling up of course, and two little white bodies came barrelling out of the dog door and across the concrete, determined to be given a ride to wherever I was going. I felt terrible beeping my Ford Focus so they'd scamper in that direction but it gave me time to get into the garage and start the door closing again. They glared at me from the other side of the yard, knowing they'd been duped.

'Teddies, I'm so sorry,' I muttered. 'Good dinner later to make up for it.'

I unlatched the shelves, holding my breath in case it didn't work this time, but I needn't have worried. The unit opened smoothly and I pulled it closed again behind me. There was plenty of light streaming through the ceiling window at this time of day so I barely needed the desk lamp.

I settled onto the very nice chair, pushed Enter so the screen sprang to life, (and relaxed a little once it did), and opened my laptop so I could research stuff without leaving a trail the Police could follow on Isobel's iMac. Or possibly Tom's iMac.

I opened the Burkeville Bar file first. Once I'd given it a much more in-depth read than my quick squiz the previous evening, I started to shake. This was no plot for a fanciful novel. It said John Bonnington was ex-Black Ops. According to the file he was one of the 'cleaners'. I did a search on my laptop for that. An assassin who also gets rid of the body and makes it seem as though nothing has happened.

I buried my chin in my hands and stared at those awful words. The shakes got worse. Surfer John killed people? The man who'd made me tea and looked after me when I'd been upset? Who'd bothered to slosh the church-flowers bucket of water over Isobel's berries? Who'd brought the teddies a drink when I'd been sitting working at his sunny table? Surfer John who was charming to customers and wanted a house at the beach?

I wrapped my arms around my waist and stared at the screen for a while longer before reading the notes on Erik Jacobsen. OMG – they were Black Ops buddies! Retired. But still... They'd left the States, bought the Burkeville as a front, and no-one suspected a thing. Except Isobel. Or possibly Tom. And now me.

Although how had anyone got hold of information like this? It was hardly Wiki-Leaks. Maybe it was Fake News?

I tried very hard to believe that, and to put it out of my mind.

Hoping for something more peaceful I tried the 'Soapworks' file. It was all crafting information – probably much more Isobel's thing than Tom's, although I'd not seen any new patchwork quilts or knitted throws in the old cottage. Not a hint of a recently embroidered cushion or cunningly découpaged picture frame. So why...?

There was a website link so I clicked on that. A dark-haired woman with beetling black brows stared back at me. Elsa Hudson. It could have been Alex with a medium-length bob. She was an artisan soap-maker. Avocado and olive oil soap. Peppermint and pumice soap for exfoliating rough skin. Peony and pecan. Orange, grapefruit and calendula soap, and plenty more. They sounded delicious. In fact they sounded as though they'd *taste* delicious. Well, maybe not the pumice...

So was Soapworks among the files because of Tom, who secretly knew about his teenage son? Had he always had suspicions? Had he somehow tracked Alex down?

Or was Soapworks there because of Isobel? Did she love luxurious soap? Or was she on the snoop? Had she checked on what Tom was researching? Was she possibly into blackmail?

Had she, by any awful chance, accused Tom of being a bad father and threatened to expose him? Had he then followed her into the church, thumped her on the head with that vase or a bottle of communion wine, left her in the aisle to bleed out, and escaped on a cruise liner?

But only for a week, and then he was coming back, so maybe not.

A sudden flurry of barking erupted from somewhere outside. Two yappy teddies and something a lot bigger and deeper. Were they being attacked?

I hurriedly closed my laptop, knowing the iMac would go to sleep on its own. Then I swiveled the shelves into place, peered quickly through the cobwebby window, saw nothing, and signaled the garage door to roll up.

John stood there, a skeptical expression on his face, with Fire and Ice on short leads. The teddies, knowing they were safe, were darting up close, growling, and then skipping out of the way again.

"You gonna call off these attack dogs?" John drawled, eyes never leaving mine as I walked out of the garage and reversed the door. "What are you hiding in there you need to close the door for?"

I shrugged and tried for an innocent expression. "Just exploring. I dropped the keys inside. The 'close the door' button must have hit the concrete."

John didn't move any of his many gleaming muscles. Didn't look as though he believed me, either.

"They're sometimes touchy," I added. "I wonder if my car remote got a bump as well?" Of course it had! I'd unlocked the car to fool the teddies. I aimed it and pressed. The lights on my Focus flashed and it made its usual locking noise.

"Good thing I checked," I said nonchalantly. The teddies' heads had of course swiveled in that direction, full of hope that a ride might follow. "Are you going surfing again?"

He continued to stand there, weight resting more heavily on his left foot so one thigh relaxed and the muscles of the other pulled tight and caught the sun. He was as streamlined as an underwear model, bronzed, graceful, and possibly an assassin. I had to remember that last bit, plus the nasty fact that those two big dogs could snap the teddies' necks in a flash and then bring me to the ground an instant later.

If he let go his firm hold on those leads.

I don't know what made me do it but I pressed the 'door up' button again, stood there trying to look relaxed while John peered inside, and then I pressed the 'door down' one.

"Just a boring old garage," I said.

He finally glanced at Fire and Ice. "I brought these two for a run on the beach. Low tide. More sand. And it gets around the 'no dogs off leads' ruling closer to the village."

Huh. Well, he was a law-abiding assassin at least... And now I'd got over the shock of finding him, I saw they weren't the same shorts he'd been surfing in. These were shiny black and cut a lot higher at the sides, which I guess wouldn't get in the way of the long strides those very long legs were going to be taking on the long sandy beach.

Overcome by so much masculinity – dogs and man – I blurted, "I'm going into the village to buy meat for a curry."

John turned slightly and the sunlight flashed off his nipple ring. How had I not noticed he was shirtless until then? Maybe because he looked the same as he had the other evening. That's the excuse I'm sticking with, anyway.

"Everything's okay then?" he asked. "No delayed reaction to finding Isobel?" He stared across at the garage again still looking far from convinced I wasn't concealing something secret in there. Little did he know!

I shook my head, unable to tear my eyes away from him. "I haven't heard anything about them discovering who killed her yet. I'll feel better once someone's locked up for it."

A gleam of sanity finally found its way past the muscles and nipple ring and short shorts. "Why have you come all the way along here for a run? There's sand across the road from you in Burkeville."

He didn't bat an eyelid. One cool customer for sure. "But no pretty ladies to check on," he said, turning, clicking his tongue at the dogs, and loping away through Isobel's garden and down the slope to the beach.

I stood there like I'd been turned to stone. Couldn't move anything except my hungry eyes which of course followed him avidly all the way. "Did you hear that, teddies?" I croaked once I'd recovered from the possible compliment. Itsy and Fluffy had both lost all their courage the moment John had given the Shepherds permission to move and were now pressed in behind my ankles. "Pretty ladies."

I walked slowly across to the garage again, thinking about that. I wasn't going to 'do an Isobel' and dash away leaving the shelves unlocked, so once I was sure John was really gone I put the garage door up again, grabbed my laptop, slid the latch home to lock the shelves, rolled the door down yet again, and high-tailed it into the cottage for my bag. His comment about 'pretty ladies' kept running through my mind. Not just one of them. Not just me. Maybe not even me at all. The pleasure of it started to diminish.

I snorted out a breath like a fire-breathing dragon, uncertain whether to be angry or not, and looking forward to a good savage session of pounding up curry spices as a stress-reliever.

I drove slowly past the entrance to Drizzle Farm in case anyone was visible from the road. Luck was on my side. Lord Jim Drizzle was stumping toward his rural mail-box with a black and white Border collie. Not fast progress from either of them, so I stopped and lowered the windows a little to make sure the teddies could breathe but couldn't follow. I really didn't fancy mud all over the seats of the Focus. Their little faces and bright dark eyes reproached me through the glass, and I could practically feel the death-rays hitting my back as I walked across to the farm gateway.

"Uncle Jim!" I exclaimed, seeing it had gone down well yesterday.

"Little Merry," he boomed.

"Not so little these days," I replied with a rueful grin. "Look – about the lawn-mowing. I found a solution but thought I'd better check it out with you. Your Alex phoned and offered to do the job for a bit of pocket money. Is that all right with you?"

Jim scratched his neck. "Not a worry." He bent and gave

the collie an affectionate scratch as well. "Good to keep the lad occupied."

"I don't want to steal him if you need him for other jobs."

"The more we can find for him, the better," Jim surprised me by saying. "He's not 'mine' in any sense of the word. I found him in the village a couple of days ago. I'd just collected Lizzie from Lisa." He gave the dog a couple of hefty pats. "And she was waiting for me outside the café."

I had visions of Lisa the vet waiting until he added, "I'd tied her to the seat by the old oak tree for a few minutes. When I came out young Alex was squatting there and giving her neck and ears a good going-over. I told him Lizzie could take any amount of that and sat down and took the weight off my feet for a while." He pulled the brim of his hat lower against the sun. "The lad's a bit lost. His mother's here for some sort of conference and he's bored silly."

"A conference? What sort of conference gets held in Drizzle Bay?" St Agatha's is the only large building with seats, and they plainly weren't holding a conference there when Isobel met her untimely death.

"Some sort of arty-farty thing," Jim said. "Patchwork quilts and pressed flowers and so on."

"Soap making?" I suggested, as a prickle of excitement ran up my spine.

"Possibly. Home-made gifts for Christmas, according to Alex. At Betty McGyver's old place. With caravans, and camper vans, and so on." He bent and gave the dog a few more thumps and she looked up at him adoringly. "So I asked if he wanted to come back here and earn a bit of money for the week. Thought it might keep him out of mischief. My last lad's moved on to learn about avocados."

Wanting to deflect Jim from thinking I was being unduly curious about the craft conference, I asked, "Has Jasper put a back on that seat around the oak tree yet?"

Many of the Drizzle Bay-ites had objected to the Roading Authority's suggestion of cutting down the out-of-place oak, and one night 'someone' had ringed the knobby trunk with a circle of seating and attached it so firmly its future was safe. Jasper Hornbeam was the number one suspect – a rebel from way back and very handy with a hammer and saw. He'd told me once there was one like it in Hampstead when he'd been a teenager. It's many, many years since Jasper was a teenager and almost as many since he left Hampstead for the antipodes so it might be gone by now.

"No – lumpy as ever," Jim confirmed. "He could do it for the village for Christmas."

"If it was really him who did it in the first place," I suggested.

Jim slapped his knee and gave a wheezy laugh. We both knew no-one else was likely to have built the seat.

"Anyway, make use of Alex if you can," he added. "I first met him and his mum a few years ago when they were passing through on their way to somewhere further north. She's brought him up on her own and done a good job. Not a conventional upbringing for sure, but he's turning out well."

Lord Jim was no fool. If he thought that, it must be true.

"Thanks for the offer," I said. "That's a big plot of land for a little woman like Isobel to try and keep tidy."

"Or anyone on their own," I agreed. "I'm sure she must have had help."

I suddenly wondered if Tom Alsop was the source of the help. Not personally of course. A full-of-himself car dealer wasn't likely to clip lavender bushes and yank out huge spent hollyhocks and chop them up for the compost heap, but he might have ensured someone else did – and perhaps paid them so Isobel kept quiet about the cars and the Asian people... or something. Well, no need to do that any longer.

"Don't suppose you have Alex's phone number, do you?" I asked with no hope at all.

Jim looked at me as though I'd suggested he sniffed cocaine.

"When you see him, can you give him this and ask him to call me?" I dug in the pocket of my jeans, found one of my business cards, and handed it over. Very smart if I do say so myself. Pale grey with faint random white letters on the background and my details in black over the top of them.

Merilyn Summerfield, Accurate Editing.

No-one ever calls me Merilyn.

"Do you do any ghost-writing?" Jim asked, hopeful eyebrows climbing his forehead.

"Not really, Uncle Jim."

His eyebrows descended again. "Thinking of an autobiography," he said. "For the family, mostly. Memoirs. History of the farm, and the House of Lords, and my early days in racing."

Anyone less Formula One-ish I've yet to meet. "Cars?" The penny dropped – or I thought it had. "Oh – racehorses!"

"Motor cycles," he said with a far-away expression. "Speedway bikes. Best days of my life. The farm four-wheelers aren't a patch on them."

It was bad enough imagining old Jim, closing in on eighty, bouncing around the paddocks on a quad bike. The image of him in one of those old-fashioned bowl-topped helmets with the leather strap buckled under his chin, hitting 100 mph or whatever they did, was terrifying.

"Wore one of those Marlon Brando jackets," he mused. "The one like he had in that movie, The Wild One. With the diagonal zipper."

I had no idea what he was talking about, but nodded anyway.

"Still got it," he said with a definite smirk. "One of my granddaughters wants it. Calls it 'a vintage classic'. Not a show I'll be parting with it."

I grinned along with him. "You could make a start on your autobiography by doing a rough outline. Even if it's just a list of chapter headings?"

"Might be enough to finally get me going on it," he agreed. "But if I wrote it, can I get you to edit it? Shove it into shape? Tell me if I'm on the right track?"

I nodded agreement. "That's exactly what I do."

"Okey-dokey," he said, turning his head towards the

distant revving roar of a chainsaw. "What are those young devils up to now?" he grumbled. "Excuse me, Merry. Need to make sure they have their safety gear on."

I gave him a brief wave as he plodded away, then I headed back to the waiting teddies who told me what they thought of being left behind in the car.

"Be quiet and I'll buy you a nice dog roll," I told them as I fired up the engine. "I can get that at the village butchery while I buy the meat for the curry. Or maybe you'd rather have something in a can, or those pretty little foil packs? Beef, or chicken, or with vegies mixed in?" I'd done a quick search online and I already knew quite a lot because of the spaniels. There'd been nothing but kibble in Isobel's pantry and surely they'd enjoy a change? "But not that organic stuff," I warned them. "It costs a fortune. We're slumming it here because I might have to pay for the lawns."

No-one answered with anything sensible and they gradually fell silent as I progressed up Drizzle Bay Road, past the vet clinic, the blueberry orchard, and the depot that sold plumbing supplies and agricultural tanks. I found an angled park in the main street of the village and once again cruelly confined the teddies to the car, this time with a view of Bernie Karaka's meat-filled window. A band of curving black and red Maori design decorated the top of the glass. Huge dog-rolls hung on strings – far too big for two little Bichons. They'd take a month to get through that, so I decided on the one-meal foil packs from the mini-mart instead. Margaret wouldn't mind paying.

Bernie the butcher greeted me with his customary broad smile, teeth gleaming against his bronzed skin, and said he had a 'nice end of rump' I might be interested in. I knew from past experience it would be so well hung it was in danger of rotting off the hook in the chiller, and would therefore be absolutely delicious. For me, alone. Not to share.

"Sold," I said, delighted. "And something to curry, too, please."

He surveyed the neatly arranged trays of cutlets and sausages and steaks in his window display and then headed for the chiller. The door swung open with a squeal, and cool air laced with meaty aromas wafted out. "Leg of lamb?" he called over his shoulder. "Or chuck?" I heard metallic clanking noises and he emerged grasping two big meat hooks – one threaded through the lamb shank and the other with a long strip of beef. "Plenty of flavor in this," he said, thumping it down on his well-worn butcher block. It seemed I was buying the chuck because he hung the leg of lamb on the hefty rail at the rear of the shop. "Get to your rump in a sec," he added, sliding a vicious-looking boning knife and steel from the butcher's pouch hanging from his belt. He gave them a few swipes together – enough to make the hairs on the back of my neck stand up – and added chattily, "I hear you found the body?"

9

BERNIE THE BUTCHER

NOT GOOD TIMING, Bernie!

I cleared my throat. "Yes, the vicar and I walked into the church together. We'd been talking outside while Isobel was arranging the flowers. He thought she was taking a long time and wondered if she was all right."

I watched as the blade flashed through the meat, cubing it up as though it was marshmallow-soft. At least no-one had taken a knife to poor Isobel.

"She was lying in the aisle," I added. "And they think someone hit her on the head with the big church vase because it was broken to bits all around her."

Bernie Karaka is the chattiest person in the world, so having told him this I could expect he'd spread it far and wide without me having to endlessly repeat the story.

He turned the meat on the block and attacked it from a better angle. "At least that's the murder weapon settled."

"But not the actual murderer, Bernie. They still have to find and arrest whoever did it."

He drove the knife through the chuck a few more times and the silvery blade shot bright reflections over the white walls of the shop. "Won't be a local."

"Why do you say that? I've heard some pretty interesting theories since it happened."

Bernie's black eyebrows rose. "Such as?"

Darn, I was getting into gossip and speculation now, and knew I'd better watch my tongue. "Well, this is all just people putting up hare-brained suggestions. Things like she laundered money for... er... drug-smugglers as well as doing tax returns. That she was blackmailing people because of what she knew about their finances. Stupid stuff like that. I'm sure none of it will be true."

"I reckon some of the boaties will be into drug-smuggling," Bernie said without blinking. "Easy money. Collect it at sea, bury it on the beach at night, someone else digs it up and distributes it. I've often thought about it."

My jaw dropped so far I could have caught flies, had there been any not already sizzled to death by the nasty ultra-violet zapping machine in the corner. *"You?"*

Bernie slid a square of waxed paper onto the tray of the scales and piled the steak onto it. "Not about *doing* it, Merry. Just the logistics. There's not much money in the shop these days. Good thing I don't have a boat, eh?" He waved his knife at the pile of meat. "That enough for you?"

I peered at the heap of neat cubes. "I was thinking twice for me, twice for Graham."

"Need a bit more, then." The knife got going again.

"And the end of rump," I reminded him. "It's very good of you to keep it for me."

(What woman worth her salt doesn't know how to butter up the butcher?)

Bernie noted the price of the chuck on the corner of a sheet of brown paper with his non-roll builder's pencil. He dived into the chiller again and returned with the saddest piece of meat you can imagine. Curled up and shrunken. Covered in lumpy yellow fat. The color of old mahogany. He proceeded to trim away plenty of the fat, sliced the meat into a small steak and one that was barely palm-sized, tossed the hook-holed end into a bin hidden under the counter, and set the treasure onto another piece of waxed paper on the scales. "That," he said, licking the corner of his mouth, "was going home with me tonight if no-one came in who'd appreciate it."

I rolled my eyes at him, with a bit of eyelash-batting thrown in for good measure. "Bernie – have I done you out of your dinner?"

He pursed his lips. "There's more where that came from. You deserve a treat after what you've been through."

"Yes," I agreed. "It's going to be a long time before I forget seeing her. If ever."

He pulled the sheet of brown paper into the center of his counter, dumped the chuck steak onto it, and laid the end of rump much more respectfully on top before glancing out at the car. Two small white faces with black eyes watched our every move, paws on the dash, noses as close to the glass as they could get them. "A treat for the main mourners," he said, selecting a pre-cooked sausage from the tray labelled 'tonight's barbecue ideas'. He rolled the whole parcel up and taped it closed. "I bet they're missing her. What'll become of them?"

I shook my head as I paid with my credit card. "No idea. I guess it's the sister's decision. Unless there's any provision in Isobel's will for them. Always supposing she had one. I can ask Graham if he knows, although he might not tell me."

Bernie gave the teddies a more thorough inspection. "I don't see Tom Alsop wanting them. Not big enough or showy enough for him." He hesitated. Rolled his bottom lip in over his teeth. Shook his head, and finally spoke. "My wife Aroha's been trying to talk me into getting a small dog but I can't stand the thought of a puppy messing everywhere. And Lurline at the shelter only seems to get big ones to try rehoming."

"Those two are beautifully house-trained," I assured him. "But I hope they wouldn't be split up." I was growing really fond of them myself, but not with two spaniels as well. "Tom and Margaret are currently away on a cruise to Fiji or some-where. As soon as the funeral's done with, I could ask?"

"They'll be worth a bit," Bernie said, gloom descending over his features. "I can't pay a fortune, not the way the econ-omy's currently doing."

I nodded. "But asking costs nothing. See you again soon." I zipped the parcel of meat into my shopping bag. Manny and Dan had taught me what a good idea that was after a couple of disasters.

The teddies welcomed me back to the car with a storm of yapping, a lot of sniffing, and sighs of resignation when no food was forthcoming. I caught Bernie watching us through the window. "New Daddy," I said, pointing him out to the little dogs. "You'd like that, wouldn't you, darlings? I can't think of anything better than being a butcher's dog."

Itsy may have given a small wuff. Fluffy flopped down on the seat and hung his nose as close as possible to my shopping bag.

Off I went to the mini-mart to collect a few groceries. I was using any excuse I could to delay phoning Bruce Carver, but at least I wouldn't be able to see his bitten nails or smell his awful cologne through the phone.

As soon as we reached home the spaniels welcomed the teddies with barks of glee, and they all went dashing around the lawn together while I lugged the groceries inside and sorted them out on the kitchen counter.

I cast about for something else to do. Gather up some different clothes! But it took a bare five minutes before I had them in the car. Oh well, nothing for it now. I needed to get over-scented Bruce out of the way and then I could have a nice time messing around with my curry. His card was pinned up on the kitchen corkboard so I gave in and tapped out his number.

"Carver," he barked.

Well darn, I'd been hoping to leave a brief message and get it done that way. It was a shame I didn't have Marion Wick's number instead. She was a lot easier to talk with.

"Yes, It's Merry Summerfield," I began. "I don't suppose you know who killed Isobel Crombie yet?"

Good start, Merry. Of course he's going to tell you.

He cleared his throat, and, anticipating cutting comments I dived in again hoping to beat him there.

"My lawyer brother told me something interesting last night," I said. "And although it's none of my business, I thought you should know."

A brief silence while he digested my news. "The public's help is always appreciated." Boy did *that* sound like a standard line he'd trotted out thousands of times.

I took a deep breath, grateful he was only on the end of the phone line. "I asked Graham if he knew who would own the cottage at the Point now Miss Crombie's dead. Someone wants to buy it. Or maybe sell it."

"And who would that be, Ms Summerfield?"

I gulped. I didn't want to throw any more suspicion on assassin John. "Just realtors. But that's not what I wanted to tell you. The cottage was willed to both sisters after the death of the parents. Nothing surprising there."

"Yeeeees.... " His patience was only going to last so long.

"The parents had their will prepared by Graham's practice long before he took over. Way back when the Crombies had been married only a year or so. They left everything to each other and then to their only daughter after they passed on. They never got around to including the second girl."

"But the will was changed to include her at some stage? Obviously it was, if the cottage was left to both sisters."

"Yes, but only a few months ago," I added quickly. "Graham told me – and please don't let this get back to him – that Margaret and Tom Alsop came into his office, each holding the elbow of one of the parents. Almost as though they were making sure they got it done. Graham said they looked so old and frail he didn't make them walk as far as the boardroom, which would have been normal for a group that size. He got his secretary to bring extra chairs into his office."

Carver digested that for a few seconds. "So you think the will was changed under duress?"

I'd really done it now. I scrambled to reverse the tone of things. "Not necessarily. You'll have to find a diplomatic way of asking Graham. He said Isobel wasn't there. Just that it was the parents who'd made the original will and they wanted to correct an oversight."

"And the main new beneficiary made sure it happened."

I fanned my face, kind of wishing I'd never rung him. "Does that seem suspicious to you?"

He cleared his throat. "It's entirely possible the parents decided for themselves, and their daughter and son-in-law simply drove them there. And assisted them into the building if their mobility was impaired."

"So why wasn't it both *daughters*? Why was Tom part of the act?"

"Act?"

"Bad choice of words," I said quickly. "The whole thing just feels wrong to me."

"Did it feel wrong to your brother?"

"Not necessarily. It was me who asked him, not him who told me, if you see the distinction. Look, maybe forget I ever raised it."

"Hold on, hold on," DS Carver snapped. "Sorry to keep on with the questions but you were absolutely right to ring me, and I'll definitely take it further. I know you're heavily invested in having this solved, given you found the deceased. Perfectly understandable. In return for that information I'll throw you a small bone."

What? Am I a dog?

"Two minutes longer," I heard him snap as though I wasn't the only person he was trying to juggle. Then he was back to full volume. "We don't think the broken vase was the murder weapon. No blood or brain matter detected on any of the fragments."

I shuddered.

"I'm telling you this in absolute confidence, and probably shouldn't tell you at all, but if it keeps you alert and co-operative I think it's a fair trade."

Hmmm. "Of course I'm co-operative," I said, thinking guiltily of all those computer files I hadn't admitted to finding yet. "If I suss out anything else, I'll let you know."

Tomorrow.

My face was burning. Good thing he couldn't see me.

"Thank you Ms Summerfield.... Merry. A pleasure to hear from you," he said in a much softer voice.

OMG – that wasn't an attempt at flirting, was it?

I disconnected, and surveyed the rest of the curry ingredients. Would Graham be home at the usual time? I phoned his longtime secretary, Mrs Henderson. Well, she was Jenny but Graham always referred to her as Mrs Henderson when he was speaking about her to other people so I tended to think of her that way, too.

"Jenny," I said chummily. "I need to tell Graham something but I don't want to disturb him." Because heaven knows the sky might fall in if he had to raise his eyes from whatever dry stuff he was wading through at this moment. "Can you give him a message please? Curry in the oven – enough for tonight and tomorrow. I'll leave it on low, and it'll be ready when he gets here. But if he wants to go off somewhere after work he'll need to duck home and switch it off."

"He'll be home at the usual time," Jenny said with calm certainty. "He mentioned the spaniels were terribly hungry when he got there after Rotary last night."

Or were putting on a good act, I thought to myself.

"That's fine then. I'm pet-sitting at Isobel Crombie's cottage out at the Point. Therefore not home to keep an eye on things for him."

"He told me." She dialed back her volume to confidential. "Have they arrested anyone yet?"

"Not so far. I was just on the phone to DS Bruce Carver and he says not."

"I'm betting it's something to do with the drugs."

Oh not again!

"What have you heard, Jenny?" All these drugs-on the-beach-at-night stories were doing my head in, but if I was now semi-officially working for the Police I felt I should explore every avenue on their behalf.

"That motor bike gang and the marijuana," she said.

I almost exclaimed 'What?' but my mother would have chimed in again.

"You be careful out there on your own," she added. "I heard she used her big garden to conceal it among the other plants. And then supplied it to the Sand Knights."

I took a surprised breath. "I really don't think so. The vicar and I had a walk around the property to check for damage after that big downpour, and surely he would have recognized it. He's quite a keen gardener. And John Bonnington from the Burkeville Bar and Grill comes along here to go surfing and running. He's from California, and I think if anyone would know about it, it's him."

There – let her assume what she liked about all my hand-some visitors!

"You don't think it's true then?" She sounded disap-pointed.

"I don't think there's the least possibility. I'll have another good walk around the garden later and search for any. I know what it looks like."

In fact I had a silver pendant of a cannabis leaf on a chain which I occasionally used to wear to annoy Graham.

And I won't admit to anything further. We were all very young once, weren't we? Anyway, if they change the cannabis laws like they're threatening to, the whole thing might go away.

I got back to the curry, thinking fondly of my mother (who always used packet curry powder.) I pounded the cardamom, coriander seeds, cumin and cloves together with my granite mortar and pestle, grinding the mixture until it was almost dust. That got rid of some of my pent-up energy. The onions and garlic were soon sizzling in the big cast-iron casserole, and I stirred in the spices, added the meat, and gave it a few minutes to brown.

I should tell you we're not traditional curry eaters. Anyone from the subcontinent would certainly roll their eyes at the addition of sieved apple baby food and sultanas and some of the other things the late Sally Summerfield used to add to it. But it tastes delicious, and Graham expects it to pretty much match the way his mother made it, so that's what he gets.

Eventually I spooned some into a plastic storage box to take with me, added extra stock to Graham's half, and pushed the casserole into the pre-heated oven. It smelled fantastic. My cheese on toast lunch suddenly seemed a long way in the past.

"Hi-ho, hi-ho, in search of hash we go," I couldn't help mumble-singing as I gathered up the rest of the groceries, the storage box of curry, and my phone.

The teddies needed no urging to hop into the Focus. The

spaniels needed a firm hand to prevent them from following. And so we bowled along Drizzle Bay Road in the curry-scented car, me occasionally belting out my stupidly amended Seven Dwarfs ditty, and the two little dogs accompanying me with random whines and howls. I don't think they enjoyed my enthusiastic singing.

Okay, clothes in the bedroom, curry in the oven, precious steak in the fridge, kettle on the boil, and out I went on my botanical expedition. Nothing in the vegie plot. Nothing in the flower borders. Nothing I could see lurking anywhere among the beachy shrubs. Jenny was way off beam with her theory.

I went inside and made tea, slightly relieved there was no likelihood of leather jacketed, prison-tatted gang members on noisy Harleys invading the place to do any harvesting.

I needed a few minutes of tranquility after all the twists and turns my life was taking so I sat at Isobel's old kitchen table and enjoyed the tea for a while.

What with one thing and another I was falling behind with my work. I had the delicious choice of editing a catalogue of light fittings which had been roughly translated from Cantonese and needed a thorough check and tweak... a collection of children's stories about two blackbirds by a charming but dyslexic woman for whom I'd edited several books previously... and a pseudo-literary novel set near Chernobyl which detailed the slow onset of radiation sickness and eventual suicide of the heroine.

Who would want to read that? (Except me, for money,

and maybe the author's mother?) The lighting catalogue would be boring but easy enough. The kiddie stories would take time but be fun. The Russian epic would be depressing and a hard slog – and worth a lot more than the other two put together.

I squared my shoulders and opened my laptop with a gusty sigh; Chernobyl here we come.

Itsy and Fluffy knew dinner time wasn't nearly due but they rattled the last pieces of kibble from their dishes to remind me their plates were as empty as their tummies. Then they settled down in the dotty dog bed with sighs as despairing as mine.

Somewhat later there was a knock on the door. I jumped a mile.

10

PAUL'S UNFORTUNATE PROBLEM

"Merry, it's me."

I jerked out of my trance of concentration and sat bolt upright. Both the teddies scrabbled from the dog bed and got stuck trying to be first through the dog door. Excited yapping and growling somehow settled the impasse while I hauled my brain out of Russia and back to Drizzle Bay.

Was that Paul? I wasn't expecting him. Hadn't heard his car. I wondered what he wanted at... I glanced at my watch... 7.30?

Where had the time gone? It wasn't a case of the book being any good. Much more that I'd been working so hard almost three hours had whizzed by.

I stood and stretched, feeling about as old and stiff as Isobel.

Unfortunate description, Merry!

"Paul," I said, as I opened the door. I was delighted to have the diversion.

He looked past me to the laptop and notepad and empty cup on the table. "I'm interrupting. Sorry. I thought if I left it until now you'd have your dinner out of the way and I wouldn't be too unwelcome." His long straight nose sniffed up the curry aroma. The forgotten casserole was visible through the oven window.

"Ooops!" I exclaimed. "It's only on low. It should be okay."

I swung the kitchen door fully open. "Come in and take a seat while I check it. It's not even for tonight."

"But you've eaten?"

I searched for Isobel's old padded hessian oven gloves, turned the oven off, and pulled the curry forward. "No – it's way past time I did, but dinner will be quick enough. I'm amazed the dogs didn't remind me."

Having presumably done their business outside, Itsy and Fluffy rattled back in, right on cue. They went straight to their dishes and sent me reproachful stares when they found nothing there.

"Hang on, doggies," I said. "New treat tonight. In fact Bernie sent you something too." I grabbed the cooked sausage, snapped it in half, and deposited some in each plate. Oh yes! Little jaws got going and made short work of that.

Then I reached for one of the foil packs – Beefsteak and Barley, although it was more likely minced lungs than anything truly steaky. "Can you rip that open please?" I asked Paul, indicating the notch at the top of the packet. I handed him a spoon and turned aside to gage the true state of the curry. Sally Summerfield would have been impressed. Bubbling gently and nowhere near dry. I pulled it out of the oven and left the lid off so it would cool faster.

Meantime the teddies were so keen to get at the food they had it all over their faces because they were trying to lick it up while Paul was trying to spoon it out.

"Are they always this hungry?" he asked.

I felt slightly guilty given what the time was, but said, "New food. Isobel only had dry kibble in the pantry so I thought they'd like a change." I bent and rummaged in the pot cupboard for a heavy frypan and switched the front burner on.

He inspected the pack. "It says single serve."

"For what size dog?"

"Small to medium."

I looked down at the teddies, who were positively quivering with delight. "Would two of them make a medium, do you think?"

He grinned. "I think they'd make two smalls. Have you got any more?"

I tossed him a packet labelled Spring Lamb and Rice.

His dark brown eyes opened wider. "They're eating better than me."

I grabbed my little parcel of yummy steak. Was I willing to share? "Have you eaten?"

"Yes, more than an hour ago," he assured me.

"Would you like a little more? I can't treat the dogs without treating you as well." I did, after all, have almost a steak and a half.

"I came to talk," he said, looking uncomfortable.

"We can talk and eat."

He gave a slow and cautious nod.

I handed him a bottle of Shiraz to open, and pointed to the shelf with the glasses. Peanut butter glasses. Isobel's tiny sherry glasses from the sitting room didn't fit the bill at all. Meantime I halved some nice big tomatoes, dropped a knob of real butter into the pan, and soon had a large and small steak sizzling noisily alongside them. I wasn't kind enough to offer him the larger steak, and I was pretty sure he would have turned it down anyway.

We ate without speaking, each of us giving occasional appreciative moans because it really was superior steak and the tomatoes hummed with flavor.

"So what's the problem?" I finally asked. He'd stayed silent, despite claiming he wanted to talk.

I sipped my wine, encouraging him with a lifted eyebrow.

"Hard to make it sound sensible," he muttered, taking a big swig of his own Shiraz. "But I wanted someone else to know about this in case it comes back to bite me."

My antennae started to twitch, so I ran my fingers back over my head to make them lie down again. Or maybe just to tidy my hair. "Okay..."

Why on earth was he looking so worried?

"It's possible," he began. Then stopped. Closed his eyes briefly. Started again. "There's a slight chance Margaret might accuse me of killing Isobel."

I practically lifted out of my chair with shock. I know my mouth opened and closed a few times like a demented goldfish. "Did you?" I squeaked. "I mean, I'm sure you didn't, but why do you think that? What grounds would she have to suspect it or to accuse you of it?"

Paul dropped his gaze to his empty plate. I'd left the steaks pretty rare, and a small puddle of blood remained on each. He tilted his up with one finger and made it slide to the side of the plate. I wished he hadn't.

"When I was in Afghanistan," he began. He flicked a glance across at me before proceeding. "I was deemed to have formed 'an unsuitable attachment' with a young private. He was gay. I'm not. He hated it there."

"Understandably," I murmured.

"And some of the men gave him a pretty hard time about being gay. He came to me for counseling, and that's the way the vicious rumors started."

Oh goodness. Poor Paul.

"You're well out of it, then. But why would that make Margaret think you might have killed Isobel?" I couldn't see how the two were the least bit related.

He took a sip of wine. Licked his lips. Set the glass down. "Because he managed to get himself discharged and followed me to New Zealand. Hung around. Became a real nuisance."

I waited while he marshalled his thoughts. I hadn't

noticed anyone new in the village, but really, why would I? I mostly had my eyes down on my keyboard in my office at home.

Paul let out a long, slow sigh. "Not so long ago, Isobel arrived to arrange new flowers out in the nave of the church while Roddy and I were arguing in the vestry. I had no idea she was there, and although I kept my volume down in case anyone came in for a few minutes' peace, he had no such qualms. He professed undying love for me and claimed I'd led him on... blamed me for not sticking up for him when he was bullied, although he totally brought that on himself with his indiscreet behavior..."

He stopped and took another sip of wine.

I supplied a few understanding nods, although I didn't understand anything much yet.

"Then he changed tack and accused me of seducing him, and betraying my professional ethics as a counsellor and my calling as a chaplain... Followed that up by threatening to kill himself if I wouldn't 'relent' and let him live with me."

Paul closed his eyes tightly for a few seconds, and then opened them again to see how I was taking things. "Rock and a hard place, I tell you. I stormed out to get away from him, and found Isobel right there. She'd crept closer to the vestry doorway so she could hear us better."

My heart was almost beating out of my chest with anguish for him. "And she probably heard plenty?"

"More than plenty. More than any good Christian would want to hear about their vicar. She bailed me up the next day – brave of her, I thought – and really went to town. Told me the parishioners wouldn't want to send their sons away on the summer camps I organized if they knew I was carrying on with such a young man. Threatened to spread the word."

"She was blackmailing you?"

He shook his head. He'd gone very pale and I knew his hand was trembling because I heard the slight shake of the glass as he set it down on the table top. "Not quite, although I wondered if she was working up to it. It must have been galling for her to have so little in the way of material things when her sister had so much."

"Apparently," I muttered.

"What? The fancy house, the clothes, the cruise and so on? She has a lot more than Isobel."

I ignored that. I wasn't certain it was all paid for. "And you think she saw this as a way of levelling the stakes between the two of them?"

Paul dropped his head into his hands. "Maybe she just really objected on religious grounds. But I was the son of a politician. She knew that. And she knew I wouldn't want my family or my church embroiled in anything like this. That's why I haven't told anyone about it earlier – even you."

Now it was my turn to take a sip of wine while I decided what to say next. The cogs in my brain were whirring furiously as I considered possibilities. "Did she tell Margaret?"

He ran a hand back through his hair. "Well, don't sisters talk?"

"Don't have one, but probably. I talk to Graham a fair bit."

"Juicy gossip," he said in a bitter voice. "Whether it's true or not."

I had no reason to disbelieve him. There was probably some way to ascertain the facts through military sources, although right now I had no idea what that might be. Find out who his politician father had been and start from there?

I thought back to when I was watching him across the road earlier in the week. He'd pushed all the right buttons for me. Surely a gay man wouldn't have attracted me so strongly? I bit my bottom lip and worried at it for a while. "Would it help... if we were seen about the village together? Man and woman stuff? A cup of coffee outside Iona's, sitting fairly close? Or we might walk the dogs down to the beach? Go to the Burkeville for a meal?" I particularly liked that last suggestion because it would be a poke in the eye for assassin John. If he really was an assassin. Somewhere in the back of my consciousness I was about as sure he wasn't as I was sure Paul wasn't gay.

Then an awful thought made me choke on my wine. I got my head down quickly so most of it landed on my empty plate, but it was a close thing. Those senior students he was planning to coach for basketball – was it a clever excuse to keep company with very young men? Rub up against them? Be physical in shorts and singlets? See them in the changing rooms or showers?

Not to stop *them* getting up to no good, after all. More likely it was him who wanted to get up to no good.

I bent, breathless, over my plate, which now looked a lot bloodier with the splatter of Shiraz.

"Merry!" Paul exclaimed as I tried to recover. He pushed his chair back, and the wooden legs scraped on the old lino. "Don't panic. Glass of water coming up."

I continued to shake my head and clear my throat and try to stifle my coughing as he put the water in front of me. A cup, rather than a glass. He'd grabbed my empty teacup.

"It's okay, I'm fine," I claimed between coughs. Plainly I wasn't because this time it was me with the shakes. The cup almost tipped over as I set it down after a sip of water. "Went down the wrong way," I said, still spluttering. "What a nasty feeling." I rubbed my throat in case it helped. It didn't.

Once I'd recovered a little I asked, "So what was his name again? Roddy something? I'd better know the whole story instead of only half. In case anyone asks."

Paul rested his elbow on the table and his chin in his hand. "Roddy Whitebottom."

I just about died, trying not to laugh. "Really?" I croaked. "Wouldn't you change your name if you were unfortunate enough to be a Whitebottom?"

Paul's lips quirked.

"Sad for a young man," I added, because it really was a tragic name to get landed with. "That'd be enough to send you gay if you weren't in the first place."

Paul looked slightly more cheerful now, although

possibly because of my unrestrained hilarity rather than any of the 'be seen together in public' things I'd suggested. "Yep," he agreed. "Doomed from day one, poor devil."

"So where is he now? Still around?"

Paul reached for my messy plate and stacked it on top of his. "Gone bush for a while but he won't be far away. He's a crack shot so he's trying his hand at hunting. Teamed up with someone else from Afghanistan. No-one I know." He shook his head.

"Maybe he'll manage to fall down a ravine or shoot himself," I suggested.

"Wash your mouth out with soap, Merry Summerfield!"

We finished off our peanut butter glasses of Shiraz. One was enough if he was driving. And one was enough so I stayed clear-headed enough for whatever my next task turned out to be.

"Anyway," he said. "Thanks for listening. And thanks for feeding me, yet again."

"Not much food though," I interrupted.

"But probably the best steak I've ever tasted."

I smiled smugly. "It pays to let your butcher show you what an expert he is." Then, to my surprise I added, "There's enough curry there for two servings if you want to turn up tomorrow?"

Paul shook his head. "You've fed me twice now. Maybe we can start reinforcing my reputation as a heterosexual?" He grinned, and raised his eyebrows. My mouth had probably fallen open. "Ms Summerfield, would you care to accompany me to the Burkeville Bar and Grill for dinner tomorrow evening?"

I sent him a flirty Princess Diana-type look from under my lashes. "In something short and clingy, vicar? So I look like a real girl?"

His grin grew broader but he said nothing. We stared at each other like a pair of fools until I nodded and amended my description. "A real *woman*, perhaps. I don't know about the short and clingy but I can definitely do low-cut."

Paul closed his eyes.

"Dutch," I added.

"No way," he protested, opening them wide again. "I've saved enough on the baking Iona will never let me pay for to buy your dinner."

I sniffed. "Don't be ridiculous. Of course I'll pay half."

"Merry," he said with some asperity. "Does it not occur to you that I might, with my background, have funds behind me?"

I'm sure I pouted. "I don't know anything about your background. I'd hardly spoken to you until a couple of days ago."

"Yeeeeaah," he agreed, stretching the word out. "And now you're living in luxury beach accommodation."

"Phooey. *And* earning twenty bucks a day. How could I turn it down?"

Finally we gave in to the snorts of laughter we'd been trying to stifle.

"Thank you Paul. I'll make an effort to look like a *femme fatale* for you. What time?"

He pushed back his chair and stood. "Seven? I don't imagine they're booked out on week nights."

I saw him to the door. Stood there waving, with the Bichons bouncing around my feet, fully-fueled and determined not to miss out on anything.

"Well, teddies – it's a good thing you don't speak English or you'd have heard some hot stuff tonight," I said as Paul's blue sedan disappeared over the rise into Drizzle Bay Road.

What was the 'background' he'd alluded to? Who had his politician father been? Not being very churchy I'd never been the least bit curious. Apart from the name 'McCreagh' and 'English MP' I didn't know what to try searching Mr Google for.

But... England. Lord Jim Drizzle popped over there to do political things, and we'd had that chummy conversation about the book I'd edit if he ever got around to writing it. It didn't feel too cheeky to try asking him. It was now eight-twenty; was that too late to phone an elderly, early-rising farmer? Maybe the message machine would pick up if he didn't. Fortified with my big glassful of Shiraz and an invitation out to dinner I decided to give it a go.

"Good evening, Drizzle Farm," the gentleman himself answered.

"Uncle Jim – it's Merry. Is this too late?"

"Everything okay?" he demanded. It didn't seem to be too late.

"Everything's fine. No panics." (Except possibly a vicar planning to prey on the local schoolboys.)

Still, Paul had closed his eyes with definite appreciation when I'd mentioned wearing something low-cut, so that gave me hope he'd stick to praying instead of preying.

"I'm being nosy," I said. "Tell me to butt out if you like, but I'm wondering if you know who the vicar's father was? It was just a stray comment I overheard…"

From the actual vicar, actually, but I wasn't going to tell His Lordship that.

Lord Jim hummed for a few seconds while he considered. "Got it! Antony Valentine-McCreagh. Hyphenated. Died a few years ago. MP for one of those English places that starts with 'Little'. There are hundreds of them. Little Runcible or Little Silly Dale or something."

LSD, my brain supplied.

"Little Dorrit?" I suggested, trying not to think about yet more drugs.

Jim Drizzle gave his trademark wheezy laugh. I could hear him slapping his thigh, or possibly the black and white collie. "That's a good one," he said. "Yes, definitely Valentine-McCreagh. Bit of a mouthful."

Not as bad as Roddy Whitebottom.

"Thanks," I said. "That solves a mystery."

"I say," Jim said in a much more businesslike tone. "I've made a start on the list of chapters for the book. Bit of a surprise how much I want to pack in there."

"Well done!" I enthused. "As long as you don't drone on in awful detail, you can certainly cover plenty of topics."

"And if I *do* drone on too long, you'll give me what-for?"

"Absolutely, Uncle Jim. Can't bore the readers."

Somewhere in the background a kettle started to whistle. "Better go and turn that off," he said. "Don't want to disturb Zinnia. Goodnight Merry." He hung up, leaving me thinking that Zinnia Drizzle was a pretty silly name, too.

So... was I going to put my brain through more hard slog in Chernobyl or was I going to watch some telly, read a book, or play on Facebook?

My initial plans for evenings at the Burkeville – perched on a tall bar stool and hoping to attract available and interested men – hadn't become reality yet, but somehow I'd found two without trying. Both Paul and John were undoubtedly attractive. Paul had said he 'wasn't suitable husband material right now', and he still might be gay despite his protestations. John *definitely* wasn't suitable husband material and he still might be an assassin, but a girl can't complain too much after a drought like I've had recently.

And who said I wanted anything permanent? I'd had a husband for years and he'd been nothing but a waste of space.

Good start, Merry. You've still got it, babe.

11

CRAFTING AT HORSE HEAVEN

You know how things feed into your subconscious while you sleep? By the time I woke up to sunshine and the sound of loudly-swooshing waves on the beach, it was obvious what my next step should be. I'd check out the crafting conference, even though I wasn't a crafter and hadn't been invited. If you have a business card and are prepared to look interested it's amazing what people will tell you.

I stretched and yawned – careful not to kick the teddies off the bed. The spaniels would never have been allowed to take such liberties with Graham, but they probably weigh twice as much as the perky little Bichons.

Graham wouldn't be caught dead sharing his bed anyway – except with Susan Hammond. Come to think of it I hadn't seen her around for a while.

Note to self; ask Graham about Susan.

Itsy and Fluffy scooted off the bed the moment they

detected signs of life from me so I guess they thought there might be some more of last night's uber-delicious food on offer. They hurtled down the hallway, skidded into the kitchen, and stood there trembling and panting as I staggered along behind them, still rubbing my eyes and dragging my fingers through my long hair.

"You did a good job of licking each other's faces clean last evening, didn't you?" I said, peering at them in the bright light coming in past the sweet peas and new hollyhock spires. "But I don't want food all over you again." I bent and lifted their bowls into the sink to rinse them clean.

"Goodness, teddies, you got every scrap." They'd been polished to a perfect shine in the search for any last smear of Beefsteak and Barley or Spring Lamb and Rice. I gave the bowls a shake to get the water off and set them down on the counter. Itsy wriggled and snuffled and bumped against my legs. Fluffy sat, sending me a long-suffering sigh and a withering stare.

"You might look like a pair," I mumbled as I tried to pull the slippery foil packet open with wet fingers, "But I'm beginning to see you as two individuals now." The packet gave way with a sudden rip. No doubt a delicious aroma issued forth because the two little dogs began dancing on their hind legs. I spooned some Chunky Chicken and Vegetables into each bowl (whines of anticipation), added some kibble to each (moans of despair), and set them on the floor. Bits of kibble got flicked sideways in the search for the good stuff. I couldn't help but grin as I made tea for myself while they were occupied.

So. The crafting conference – if that's what it really was.

Jim Drizzle had said it was at Betty McGyver's place. A quick search took me to Old Bay Road – a rural location which looked horsey from the aerial view. Well, it had an oval training track and what might be a big barn, anyway. There was certainly plenty of room to park multiple vehicles. I'd had no reason to drive in that direction for years.

The teddies rattled out through their door and I went to have a shower once I'd finished my tea. I was soon suitably dressed in my best jeans, navy jacket and white shirt, hair up in a passable twist, with black ankle boots in case the conference venue was muddy. I slotted a slice of bread into the toaster and found the butter and marmalade. I even spotted a couple of very early strawberries when I wandered out into the sun with my plate.

Old Bay Road looked to be no more than a few minutes past the village so the teddies could stay home. After all, Isobel hadn't always taken them out with her – they'd been running free here on the day she died. That was enough to send a shiver down my spine as I swiped some more red lippy on, using the little old mirror fixed to the wall beside the fridge to check my reflection. I nearly ran off the edge of my bottom lip with that shiver.

I locked the house up and beeped the Ford Focus to unlock it, then had to convince Itsy and Fluffy they weren't getting a ride to anywhere

Huffs of disbelief. Four black eyes trying to peel the paint off the car.

Teddies, you almost have me wrapped around your little paws, but not quite.

"I won't be long," I assured them through the cracked-open window. I'm sure they appreciated the information.

It took almost no time to get to the venue once I was through the village. I swooped up a couple of very green hills, dived down the valleys that followed, and then had to stop to give way to someone on a one-way timber planked bridge. The view sideways showed me a sparkling slice of Drizzle Bay with Brett Royal's whale-watching boat plowing out on its morning tour. I rattled on over the bridge and soon turned in through white gateposts beside a sign saying 'Horse Heaven'.

Anything less like a conference I'd never seen. Two caravans, a couple of camper vans, one olive green bus with curtains, a horse cantering along beside the fence as I crawled up the graveled driveway, and ten or a dozen women doing tai-chi in the sun.

They turned briefly in the car's direction and then ignored me. Either my arrival had speeded up the end of the class or they were almost finished, because within sixty seconds they broke ranks and all but one of them ambled into the building I'd assumed from the aerial shot was a barn. It definitely looked like a barn now I was at ground level. The air smelled of straw and dung and... bacon!

The woman who'd walked toward me stopped. Older

than me, with curly grey hair and fawn cargo pants covered in spots and splatters of dried-on white goo. She reached out a hand to shake, and her blue eyes assessed me keenly. "I'm Betty. And you are?"

"Merry Summerfield." I already had my business card out of my pocket for her.

She gave it a very quick appraisal. "Editing? We're into handcrafts, not mind-work."

I shook my head. "I haven't come to join in, exactly. But I was talking to Jim Drizzle yesterday..."

Good – a definite flicker of interest.

"And he told me you were doing this, and I wondered if you'd allow me to write it up for a tourism blog I sometimes contribute to."

That wasn't entirely dishonest. Or entirely honest, either. During my worst days with Duncan Skeene I'd tried writing travel pieces to distract myself. I'd had several published, but more as a 'guest without payment' than as any sort of expert. If Betty insisted, I could scroll through to items on my phone about a wine tasting trip to Marlborough and a beach ramble that included the amazing huge round Moeraki boulders on the coast of the South Island – each with a tiny photo of me as author. However, it seemed she was prepared to take me at my word. "Come and have breakfast," she said, beckoning me into the barn.

That bacon did smell amazing so I decided not to admit to my slice of toast and marmalade until I saw what else was on offer.

By an open window on the far side of the barn I spotted the familiar lanky figure of Alex flipping thick slices of bacon and toasting whole-wheat buns on a big stainless steel barbecue. He caught sight of me and I opened my mouth to greet him but he gave one sharp shake of his head. Okay then... doesn't know me. Or not in front of the craft ladies, anyway. And, I guess, definitely not in front of his mother.

I turned away from him and gazed around the rest of the barn. Trestle tables formed a rough horseshoe and each was topped with arty items. There were a dozen or so chairs around one and I assumed they got dragged from table to table depending on what was happening. Right now breakfast was happening.

"Best breakfast I ever saw at a conference," I said to Betty, inhaling the heavenly smell of freshly cooked bacon. Whoever had cut it up was very generous.

She smiled, showing a glint of gold in one tooth. "Don't call it that," she said. "We're not a conference. We're barely a seminar. We're kind of a pow-wow."

"A power-wow," I said, unable to resist the play on words. "A group of strong women sharing ideas and skills."

"Exactly," she agreed, handing me a plate with a bacon-filled bun. And I do mean *filled*. Maybe I should have turned it down when she first offered. But... let's call it brunch instead of breakfast.

She grabbed her own plate and ushered me to the table. There was an enormous teapot, a liter of milk, and a pottery bowl of sugar making their way down the center. I poured myself a cup as things reached me.

Betty clinked her teaspoon on the side of an empty mug and its chime quietened everyone down. "Listen up, people, this is Merry. She's aiming to get us some free publicity."

There was some surprised murmuring, most obviously from a woman with a sing-song Welsh accent who asked, "Why would you do that?"

Betty put her bun down on her plate. "Phyllis-Elizabeth! Merry's come to us through Lord Drizzle, and they're both keen to see local projects do well. If we could get an extra influx of customers to the handcrafts stall on Saturday morning I'm sure we'd all be very pleased." She looked back to me. "She writes poetry," she muttered.

"Phyllis-Elizabeth Robertson," the woman said, holding out a hand to shake as though she was famous. "I also knit bathmats. Chunky pure cotton – very absorbent."

I nodded, thinking to myself you could buy a normal toweling one for less than ten bucks on special. How many did she sell after all those hours of knit one, purl one?

"What about that murder?" the goth-looking girl at the end of the table suddenly exclaimed. "It won't do the place much good."

A babble of speculation followed, including comments from Phyllis-Elizabeth about being careful to lock vehicles at night.

I wondered whether I should tell them about finding the body. Noooo... better not. "Where are you having the stall?" I asked Betty, hoping to get the conversation back on track. I took another bite of the truly amazing bacon. Sweet and succulent, and caramelized along the barbecued edges. Maybe it had been cured with Manuka honey?

"Opposite the church where the murder was. Outside the café. Iona's willing for us to use two of her tables if we add a couple more. Quid pro quo. We'll be attracting customers for her, providing we don't get in her way."

I made a show of tapping out a few notes on my phone and then looked around the table. "So what do the rest of you do?"

Barely stopping for breath, Betty dived in again. "I crochet. Infinity scarves, baby booties, anything that takes my fancy, and all with hand-spun wool from the farm. And I decoupage boxes and trays. We had my workshop yesterday, which is why we're all covered in glue." She glanced down at her spotty trousers and I grinned back at her.

"Button art," the large woman next to her said. "Wall hangings, necklaces, other jewelry. I'm Jessie."

Now I looked at her more closely I saw she wore colorful earrings which were indeed made from stacks of threaded buttons. "Very creative," I said, pointing at her ear with the hand not clutching my bun.

"Clothes-peg zombies," goth-girl said. "Walking Dead kind of characters."

"Thoroughly spooky," Phyllis-Elizabeth said with a shiver.

"*Meant* to be," goth-girl insisted. The silver ring through her black-glossed lip twinkled in a shaft of morning sunlight. I presumed teenagers would go for her ghoulish ornaments, but I wasn't so sure I would. "And I tie-dye T-shirts," she added. "I'm Zee."

"Patchwork," an older woman with hennaed hair said. "Quilts and waistcoats mostly." At least that sounded fairly normal.

"I paint stones," the next woman murmured.

"Beautiful flowers and fruits for paperweights and garden ornaments," Betty explained. "And she sometimes makes name-markers for rows of seeds. You hide your light under a bushel, Rachel."

Rachel gave half a shrug and half a smile.

The next woman was Alex's mum. "Handmade soap," she announced. Her hair was longer and much wilder than in her website photo, but her eyebrows were unmistakable.

"I'd like to buy some of that," I said, hoping I could get her talking, and still wondering why Isobel had been interested in her.

"Good for your skin. All natural ingredients." She turned her back and reached for the milk, dismissing me with her abruptness.

I transferred my gaze along the table to the next person. I say 'person' rather cautiously. His or her hair was cut soldier-short, there was no make-up in evidence, and the androgynous jeans and loose camouflage-patterned T-shirt gave no further clues. The person said in an unhelpful husky voice,

"I'm a beachcomber. I take what nature gives me and turn it into art."

I nodded, wondering what the 'art' was.

"Nic is our star," Betty said.

Unhelpful name, too!

"Winston at the gallery has some of Nic's pieces on display. Well worth a look," Betty added.

"Wonderful." I hoped I looked impressed. "Winston's no fool."

"Charges like a wounded buffalo," Alex's mum muttered, flicking a glance up over the rim of her cup.

"Are you saying my stuff's not worth decent money?" the Nic person demanded.

"Ladies!" Betty exclaimed. So that solved Nic's sex, although possibly not her proclivities. (But who am I to judge? I chose Duncan Skeene, and he chose everyone else.)

"Everything finds its own level," Betty continued. "And I really think your soap could sell for more, Elsa, but we'll be covering that in our marketing segment." She turned to me. "No point charging too little for something so beautifully made." She took a bite of her bacon-filled bun. "He was a lovely pig, our Harold," she added.

I felt a bit faint at that. Could you eat something you knew the name of? I found I could after another tentative bite. Yes, Harold was delicious. "I daresay he had a happy life here," I suggested.

"All the windfall apples from the orchard," Betty said.

"And Bob Peyton's pears when they dropped over the fence."
She waved a hand toward the open doors of the barn. "Anyone
who lives here gets everything good we can give them."

Okay then. Best I could hope for, really.

"Anything from leather," the next woman said when I
looked enquiringly at her. "Plaited or knotted or sewn. I'm
not fussy."

"More patchwork." That was the dark-haired girl beside
her. "Mine's all smaller things – bags and cushion covers and
so on. With lots of lace and ruffles."

I nodded, watching out of the corner of my eye as Alex
shut down the barbecue. Then I turned to Betty again. "I'm
wondering how much use my publicity can be when your
stall is only a couple of days off. What else have you got
planned?"

The tubby button art lady giggled. "We'll be trotting
around the streets taping notices onto fences and lamp-posts
early on Saturday morning."

"Because," Betty said, possibly turning pink, "we haven't
applied for a sidewalk permit to hold the sale."

"It'd eat up all our profits," the red-haired patchworker
said. "We're reckoning no-one in authority will be able to get
there to close us down by the time we've already done it and
gone away."

I joined in the general laughter. They were probably
right. Certainly WPC Moody and PC Henderson and their
mates would have bigger fish to fry. Maybe some minor

district official would send a letter meant as a slap on the wrist but that would be about it.

"Anything I can get published could only tell people what a worthwhile event the stall *was*, but I could mention the interesting collective you have going here. How often do you get together?"

"First time," Betty said. "This is a try-out."

"But you'll be doing more?"

"Yes. You bet. Of course," they chorused.

"Maybe not all of us every time," Betty conceded. "But we thought one more weekender, closer to Christmas, and with a few extra people. Iris Cho paints beautiful cards and Emily Payne makes exquisite tree decorations, for instance." She looked across at Alex's mum. "There's no reason why you couldn't tie your soaps up with pretty loops of ribbon, Elsa, and promote them as tree ornaments. Or your lovely stones, Rachel."

She returned her attention to me. "And if this Saturday goes well, we'll pass out invitations to the next. No need for a sidewalk permit for that because we'll hold it here."

"Can I take some photos?" I asked.

"We're not exactly looking our best," the quiet stone-painter objected.

"Speak for yourself," skinny Nic sniped. I couldn't see she'd made the least bit of effort with her appearance, but that was her business.

"Maybe not *us*," Betty said, pouring some quick oil on the swirling waters. "We're all in casual gear and prepared to get messy. But how about what we make?" She rose and collected up items from the other tables. Yes, she was artistic for sure because in no time she'd created a pretty grouping out of nothing much. I took a few shots with my phone.

"Or we could... " she said, hands busy. The color scheme changed and different items were brought to the foreground of the display.

"You're good at this," I said, taking several more photos.

She smiled. "An equestrian lifestyle farmer who likes to make things look pretty," she agreed.

"Bye Mum," Alex suddenly yelled from the far side of the barn. His mother glared at him.

"Your son?" I asked, pretending to be surprised. "He does look rather like you."

She nodded, watching goth-girl who was staring after Alex with hungry, black-rimmed eyes. "Too young for you, Miss Peg-people Weirdo," she snapped. "Don't even think about it."

That wasn't very nice! Everyone ignored the comment. Even kind-seeming Betty. Strange forces were suddenly at play in the previously cheerful barn.

Twenty seconds later Alex hurtled by on a small Vespa-type motor scooter, scattering stones in all directions and assaulting the peaceful country air with the screaming whine of its underpowered engine. It looked like his big black motor cycle boots were only wishful thinking.

"Well," I said, deciding it was best to ignore the atmosphere and adding a bit more tea to my cup, "I'll see what I can do for you all. The pre-Christmas bash sounds like the one to go for. We've got a few weeks to think about that. I'll pop by and see if I can get some decent shots of the Saturday stall and maybe try for an item in the Coastal Courier." (Our unremarkable but popular local rag.)

"Can't tempt you to my button art class?" big Jessie asked hopefully. "It's up next."

I shook my head. "You've all been a nice diversion from what I really should be doing – editing a weepy novel set near Chernobyl."

That drew murmurs of doubt, distress and disbelief.

"Hard going?" Nic asked.

"Sucking the life out of me," I admitted. "And then I have the treat of tidying up a lighting catalogue that's been roughly translated from the Chinese original. You can see why I was keen to grab a bit of country air and some intelligent female company."

I took my last sip of tea as they preened at my praise.

———

AND SO I retraced my route back over the one-way bridge, up and down the hills, and into the village center again. I wouldn't need lunch after my generous portion of Harold, but I stopped at The Café and bought a carrot muffin with cream cheese icing, intending to drop it off to old Rona Jarvis in Beach Street as a treat. My plans were thwarted when I found Paul there, in shorts and T-shirt, hacking away at the very overgrown grass on her small front lawn with a genuine old-fashioned scythe. Goodness, the man had some energy! And some muscles.

I stepped out of the car and sauntered to the open gate. Unfortunately he caught sight of me before I could do much admiring. "Is she in?" I asked, holding up the muffin.

"We tracked down a sister. She's gone to spend a few days there while we tidy up."

I watched his chest rising and falling after the exertion, and then ripped my gaze back up to his face. "Looks like you deserve this, then. I handed the bag across to him. That's very medieval," I added, nodding toward the scythe.

He leaned on the long handle. "I found it in her garden shed. Never used one before. There's a definite knack to it."

"Just as well it's only a small patch."

He nodded, and opened the bag. "A lawn mower certainly wouldn't cope yet. Jasper Hornbeam's around the back, fixing some rotting steps."

"I only bought one muffin," I said, watching as he bit into it. "I'd better go and get another one for him."

Paul shook his head, and swallowed. "He brought lunch from home. He's been threatening me with a slice of cold steak and kidney pie."

I pulled the corners of my mouth down. "Might be delicious, but it's not immediately grabbing me."

"Or me. I'll go home for something in a while." He crumpled the paper bag and threw it into the old wheelbarrow where he'd been piling the stalks of grass.

"See you later, then." We'd already arranged that he'd collect me from the family home in the village for the drive to the Burkeville Bar and Grill. All my *femme fatale* clothes were there because I'd taken nothing the least bit glam to the cottage yet.

"Ten to seven." He inserted the last of the muffin and wolfed it down. "Have a good afternoon."

———

I HAD spying in mind next. First up was a search through the old cottage for any signs that Isobel had been a fan of Elsa's botanical soaps. I found nothing but Palmolive in the bathroom, or stacked in the vanity cupboard, or in her bedroom chests of drawers. I even checked the linen cupboard again in case she'd been using it to scent the sheets.

"So why was she interested?" I asked Itsy. She was sticking close, maybe hoping for more food now I was home. She put her head on one side and looked very cute but offered no help.

"Was it Tom who was spying on Elsa? Do you think he knew she'd had his son?" Itsy yawned so widely I could see all her sharp white teeth.

Although the two little dogs had been running free, I decided we all needed a walk on the beach before I began ploughing through the remainder of the Chernobyl dirge on this lovely day. I changed into shorts and flip-flops and locked the cottage. We scrambled down the incline at the end of the garden and were soon enjoying the hard-packed sand while tiny waves slid up and were sucked away again and noisy seagulls wheeled and dipped in the spring sunshine. Fluffy attempted to chase some as they waddled ahead of us but they flew up with shrieks of derision every time he got close. Halfway to the horizon the whale watch boat chugged back toward the jetty at the end of another excursion. I couldn't help wondering what sort of living Brett made from his tours, and hoped he didn't need to supplement it with midnight people smuggling or drug runs. That's the trouble with small places; gossip runs wild. I thought about that some more as I turned us around and headed home again to do some work.

Another hour in Chernobyl was quite enough. Not enough to finish the editing job but plenty to flatten my spirits. I decided on one more look through the files on the iMac before letting Bruce Carver know about them. And might there be more emails? It was easy to imagine Tom and Margaret Alsop living it up large in a Florida retirement community. Much easier than picturing Isobel. They could take their cruising clothes! The original messages had been addressed to Isobel, but this whole setup was so wacky it was anyone's guess who was impersonating who.

Once again I unlocked and re-locked the old garage, swiveled and re-swiveled the shelf, and settled into the office chair. And once again nothing really made sense. Having now met Elsa Hudson at Betty's place, the Elsa-Alex-Tom trio was far more interesting to me than anything else on offer, so

I dug around in files and notebooks that might tie them together but came up empty-handed. Or maybe I mean empty-brained.

There was one enigmatic new email from Nam Cheng. It simply said 'Tomorrow.' With Isobel dead and Tom off cruising I doubted that would be happening. I was tempted to hit Reply and say 'Not tomorrow', but it wasn't my business to make a car thief's life easier. If he really was a car thief, of course.

That reminded me I'd been going to transfer the most interesting-looking files to Dropbox, so I spent some time doing that and then tilted my head back and gazed up through the big window in the ceiling. I didn't like the feeling of being enclosed with no view except sky and occasional clouds. You'd need to really want your privacy to feel comfortable here.

I glanced at my watch and got a fright when I saw how much time had slid by while I'd been nosily sleuthing. I'd vowed to give Isobel's fruit and vegies a good watering because it had been an unrelentingly sunny day, but it was either that or feed the dogs because I needed to dash home and make myself look gorgeous for Paul. The dogs won, of course. I closed up the office, closed up the garage, and went to open the dog food. And that's when I found the next courier envelope.

12

DINNER TO DECEIVE

IT WAS LEANING against the back door of the cottage this time. Why not in the mail box?

Once again it was addressed to Tom Alsop. And once again I couldn't get it open without wrecking it. I expelled an annoyed breath and threw it on the kitchen table before feeding the dogs. Turkey and Giblet Feast. Ooops – there was a cat's face on that pack so I must have shopped in too much of a hurry. Itsy and Fluffy didn't mind at all though. Every morsel and smear disappeared from their bowls.

Then I shot off to the bedroom to collect the make-up I'd brought with me and anything else I wanted to take home. I was halfway to the village before I remembered I hadn't yet called Bruce Carver about the secret office and all the files. Oh well, later would do. He couldn't get into the garage before tomorrow morning anyway.

PAUL ARRIVED RIGHT ON TIME, looking like a younger Hugh Grant in good navy jeans and a pale blue shirt with the top button undone. The blue was very flattering against his sun-kissed skin and dark hair. The jeans threw me, though. On any other man, absolutely right for a casual meal. On the man I was used to seeing in a dog-collar? Not at all. Except... that was the whole point, wasn't it; to present him as a normal desirable male dating a woman?

The woman in question had gone to town with the make-up. Plenty of moisturizer to make up for the beach walks, rather more care than usual getting the tinted foundation even, lots of eye shadow and mascara, and my French Cherry lipstick. I'd chosen strappy pale pink sandals that were difficult to walk in, a cerise dress with a very low scoop to the neckline, and the occasional flash of black lace bra edging which contrasted beautifully with the deep pink fabric of the dress. And indeed, the pale creamy skin of my most valuable assets.

"Fffwhoaaarrrr!" Paul exclaimed in his best English accent, eyes rather wide and surprised.

I blinked. "Am I all right? Have I overdone it?"

He shook his head slowly. "Like your hair."

Not what I was expecting! I'd brushed it out so it tumbled down over my shoulders. I have so much of it that close friends sometimes ask if I have hair extensions.

No, darlings, I grew it all myself, and it's a jolly nuisance trying to get it all dry after I've washed it.

Maybe Paul had always seen it in a bun, or tied back in a pony-tail?

Or was 'like your hair' intended to convey more? He was still staring at me as though I'd leaped out of a lingerie catalogue.

Okay, this was good, but only up to a point. Yes, I looked very female. If he kept on staring at me with such appreciation no-one seeing us together would think he was anything but a red blooded on-the-rut ram. But... perhaps not too great an image for a vicar?

I dug him in the ribs. "Dial it back a bit from that?" I suggested. "Your tongue's hanging out."

He gave a rueful grin. "You've really gone for broke. I'll be fighting men off."

"Men?" I asked, with a suggestive lift of one eyebrow.

He mock-cuffed me on the chin. "Off *you*."

"More or less the aim, wasn't it? To make it look as though you had an eye for the ladies?"

Paul drew a sharp breath and closed his eyes for a few seconds. "I *do* have an eye for the ladies, Merry, and you're certainly going to reinforce that to anyone who sees us. Thank you."

"For?"

"Making such a sterling effort. I'll try not to ogle you quite so obviously, but let's just say it'll be no hardship sitting opposite you."

What a lovely man. And then it struck me how much fun it would be if John was working and saw us together, me all boobalicious and Paul all eyes on the prize.

Merry, you evil girl. You're enjoying this far too much.

Paul glanced at his watch. "Are we off?"

I suppressed my naughty thoughts, locked the house door, and minced out to the car with him. I'd bought the pale pink sandals to wear to a friend's wedding, and now I thought about it they'd been kicked off under the table the instant my painful hour of standing to chat and drink was over. I'd never been so pleased to sit down for a wedding breakfast. But they looked the part for sure, and hopefully there'd be no hour of standing tonight. I planned to have my feet under the table pretty soon after we arrived at The Burkeville.

As it turned out, my feet started well off the floor because Paul guided me across to a couple of empty bar stools, offered me his hand so I could hop up onto one without falling off, and then he slid onto the other.

The same pretty waitress I'd seen when I came to use the Wi-Fi greeted us.

"Something to drink?" she asked, possibly sending a surprised glance at my cleavage, and certainly lingering on the Hugh Grant version of Paul.

"Cranberry and lemonade, thanks."

May as well match my dress.

"A light beer for me."

Looked like we both planned to use our alcohol allowance to accompany the meal.

Imagine my glee when our drinks were carried over to us by assassin John.

"Merry," he greeted me, setting down my pink drink. "*Vicar*," he said with a lift of eyebrows and a flash of irritation from his unnerving blue eyes as he handed my friend his beer. What had Paul done to deserve that? Transformed into a handsome man escorting a young(ish) glamor-puss out to drinks and dinner, I supposed. People don't like being surprised. For all I knew John had him neatly filed away as taking groups of conservatively garbed old ladies with walking sticks to admire the stained glass windows in his church.

Not tonight, Bon Jovi!

I glanced around. No-one was too close, so I leaned forward at a far from wise angle. "While you're here, John," I said quietly, "I found out from my brother who Isobel's house will go to. It's Margaret, as you suspected."

Paul shot a surprised look at me. John grimaced.

"And it'll be a number of weeks before probate's settled and anything further can happen. Sorry."

John wiped some non-existent drips off the bar in front of us. "Thanks anyway."

"What business is it of his?" Paul demanded the moment John moved away.

"He surfs along that beach. He was interested in buying the cottage off Isobel."

"Bet she didn't want to sell!"

"No, she didn't. And it wasn't hers to sell, anyway. It was left to both sisters jointly." I was still talking very quietly. "I dug that out of Graham, but it's not common knowledge."

Paul started turning one of his shirt-cuffs back. "Lips are sealed."

I nodded, watching his long fingers turn the crisp blue fabric over and over, and his forearm with its fascinating tendons and dusting of dark hair come into view fold by fold.

"Evening Vicar," a cheerful voice boomed. We turned in unison to find Brett Royal from the whale watch boat.

"Evening Brett," Paul said, sending me the slightest of smirks.

Yes, all right, it's working. Clever me.

"Nice night for it," Brett said. "Whatever 'it' is."

"Been a good day, too," I said, ignoring his innuendo. "I saw your boat leaving this morning when I was heading to Old Bay Road. And again this afternoon from the beach."

"Need to make hay while the sun shines," Brett said. "Mostly orca out there at this time of year. The big whales migrate in the winter months, so I've created some escorted fishing trips to the good spots in case we don't see what we're after."

"Where are the good spots?" Paul asked.

Brett tapped the side of his nose. "Anywhere the fish are biting." He added his broad trademark grin and asked me, "Where was I headed?"

I lifted my glass for a sip and then stopped. "I think you

were coming back the second time. I was walking some dogs at the Point."

"Old Isobel's place? Shocker." He diverted his attention momentarily as the waitress came to take his order. "G and T for Miri, thanks, Lauren. Steinie for me." He turned back to us. "Who'd kill a poor old girl like her?"

"We'd all like to know that," I said. "Including the cops. Last time I spoke to Bruce Carver he said they hadn't made an arrest yet."

We all nodded somberly.

To my immense delight it was John who brought the drinks across again. He was cordial to Brett but definitely looked daggers at Paul. And he'd been eavesdropping. "Isobel Crombie?" he drawled. "The killer's either a certifiably crazy dude or knew something no-one else did."

"Or *thought* they knew," I said. "I've heard some ridiculous theories."

"Such as?" Brett asked, stroking the beautiful Maori bone carving that always hangs around his sturdy neck.

I took a sip of my drink. "Such as she did your tax return, decided you were people smuggling or drug smuggling on the whale boat after midnight, and she was blackmailing you for some of your spare millions."

Brett opened his eyes wider. "Good one. Wish I was really making enough for that." He seemed unfazed by the theory. "Don't forget she had a garden full of Mary-Jane," he added with a wink. "Not unheard of around here."

"No, she didn't," I said. "I checked."

"What?" Paul asked. "Why?"

"Because Brett's not the first person to mention that, and I wanted to be sure no-one was likely to turn up wanting any."

"Merry," he said, shaking his head in mock despair. Or maybe not entirely mock.

Brett gave Paul a manly slap on the shoulder. "Definitely not me. When did I last darken your doors, Vicar?"

"I doubt you could even find my church," he agreed.

"I rest my case," Brett said, reaching out for his beer and his wife's gin and tonic and ambling off with them.

Paul slid his hand halfway over mine. John's unnerving blue gaze followed.

"Does Marion Wick have any theories," I asked him.

John's eyes flashed back to mine. "Why ask me?"

"Oh," I said, pretending surprise. "I thought you had a little thing going with her."

"As you've just demonstrated with Brett, strange stories do get around."

What a cool customer. Not a twitch.

"She's very pretty."

"So are you, Ms Summerfield." And with a pointed glance at my neckline, he turned away.

"I've overdone it," I muttered to Paul. "Did you see that?"

He let go of my hand and grinned now John wasn't there to be misled by it resting on mine. "In fairness, you do have a dynamite rack."

"Rack?" I croaked.

He shrugged one shoulder. "Rack of ribs I suppose. Soldiers. Bad influence." He tucked his tongue into his cheek. "Don't worry, Merry," he whispered. "You have no ribs on display at all."

"Paul!" I protested.

His unrestrained guffaw turned quite a few heads. Just what I'd been hoping to achieve, but maybe not at my own expense.

He reached for a couple of menus from a nearby holder and handed one to me. "Want to choose your dinner? May as well get our order under way."

"Well, well!" two women chorused right behind us. "What are you two up to?"

We swiveled our heads around like guilty children. Lisa and Lurline stood there, hands on hips and accusing expressions on their faces.

"Only having dinner," Paul said, possibly going a bit pink. "I thought Merry could do with some company instead of eating all on her lonesome out at The Point."

Lisa was looking her tiny trim self in skinny jeans and a textured white cotton top. Lurline had tied her dreadlocks back with an orange ribbon that matched one of the colors in her long batik skirt. Neither appeared to believe Paul's explanation. Hopefully anyone else at the Burkeville would think the same.

"What have you done with the kids?" I asked Lisa.

"It's Ten Ton's night for 'daddy time'." She stood on tiptoe to peer at my cleavage. "I see you bought your girls out for some air." Yes, she was short, and I was perched up on the stool, but did she have to be so obvious?

I pointed a forefinger at her. "I've only worn this dress a couple of times. I want to get my money's worth." I hoped she'd think any possible pinkness on my cheeks was a reflection from the cerise fabric.

Lurline nodded and smiled. "Looks like the vicar's getting his money's worth, too."

"Lurline!" I exclaimed.

"Well, you don't let your hair down for just anyone," she said, eyes twinkling. "What else would I be talking about?" She reached over and touched my abundant mane. "You're so lucky. Mine's ultra-curly. The dreads are the only way I can deal with it."

"You could chop it off in a pixie cut like mine," Lisa said. "A vet can get seriously messy around big animals. That much hair would really hold me back."

We all laughed, no doubt picturing tiny Lisa covered in cow dung and mud.

Paul sipped his beer. "It's good Ten Ton's seeing more of the children. Boys need time with their dad."

"One weeknight plus every second weekend," she said. "It's not enough. I wish he'd come home."

"Have you told *him* that, instead of moaning to all of us?" I asked. When she looked appalled I quickly added, "It's not the first time you've mentioned it, that's all. Try asking him nicely."

"He won't."

"How do you know?"

"He just *won't*."

"Lisa," Paul said quietly. "Sometimes people outside the situation see things those caught up in it can't. What have you got to lose by asking him? At worst he'll still be gone. But at best your kids could get their dad home again and you might be able to rekindle things with him. Even if it's a bit rocky for a while."

"Sheesh," she said, raising her chin and pulling her shoulders back. "I came out for a meal, not marriage counselling or friends poking their noses in." She glared at Paul who was twice her size. Ten Ton was a lot bigger again. And I guess a mature Angus bull outweighed the whole group of us. Where did she get her fierceness from?

"Buy you ladies a drink?" Paul asked in a conciliatory tone. "Would you like to sit and eat with us if I haven't offended you too much?"

"That looks nice," Lurline said, pointing to my cranberry and lemonade.

"Brandy and ginger," Lisa snapped.

I closed my eyes for a couple of seconds. The idea had been to make it look as though Paul was out on a somewhat romantic date, not that he was so desperate to be seen with women he had to round up three of us. How gay would that look?

"No thanks to sitting together, if you don't mind," Lisa added.

I said a silent thank you.

"This is a business dinner. Lurline and I have things to talk about."

Paul inclined his head. "Maybe another time then."

"Maybe," Lisa agreed, but she still looked furious.

"Vicar!" Lurline exclaimed. "Rona Jarvis – thank you for following up. And thank you Merry for passing the message on."

Paul stared at his beer. "Right now Drizzle Bay's not safe for old ladies living alone.

Or younger ones," he added, just as the waitress approached our group. I ignored that as he placed the order for Lisa and Lurline's drinks.

"We'll be over there," Lisa said, indicating a vacant table for two. "Thank you," she tossed back at Paul as she hurried off.

"Brave of you," Lurline said to Paul. "I'll take the drinks across. You're right though – what does she have to lose?"

"Two stubborn people," I said, noticing John was now the center of attention with a group of nubile young women who looked as though they'd been poured into their stretchy clothes. "And Drizzle Bay's perfectly safe to live in. Just not safe to go to church in." Now it was me who was snappy.

Lurline rolled her eyes. "Hardly his fault. Are you two having a lovers' tiff?"

"NO," we roared.

"Could have fooled me." She picked up the drinks the waitress had just set down. "Thanks for these, Vicar."

"Paul," Paul and I corrected her in unison.

"You'll get over it," she said, departing with a grin.

I turned my gaze down to the menu and muttered to Paul. "Mission accomplished. That's John Bonnington, Lauren the waitress, Brett, Lurline and Lisa who all now think you're a ladies' man."

"And that we're having a lovers' tiff."

I glanced up at him again. There was definitely affection lurking in his dark eyes. And amusement. "Job done, then," I grumped. "For that I deserve the scallops."

"And the butterscotch ice cream and raspberries?

How did he know?

13

ANOTHER POSSIBLE WEAPON

IT WAS the nicest night out I'd had in ages. Having Paul make it clear he wasn't suitable husband material (maybe until his PTSD was less of an issue?) took the usual male/female tension out of the atmosphere and we relaxed and had a really good chat over dinner. His mother was widowed, which I already knew from my sneaky enquiries about his dad to Jim Drizzle. He had a sister called Heather who loved cooking and wanted to enter The Great British Bake-off. He had no nephews or nieces, and seemed sad about that. I didn't like to dig too deeply.

I told him about how I'd met Duncan Skeene.

"Why do you always call him by both names?"

"Do I?" I thought for a bit. "No idea. He's just a cardboard cutout called Duncan Skeene these days. Not a man I loved for long because he... didn't love me for long, either."

"But you stayed together?"

"I guess," I said slowly, "that I hoped he might change. That it wasn't really over. Stupid things like that. I stayed far too long."

"Did he need you?"

His question surprised me. "Not at all, as far as I could see."

"People like to be needed, even if it's only a little." He added at a much quieter level, "Take Lisa and Ten Ton as an example. She's so feisty and capable she's made him feel inadequate and so she's driven him away."

I tipped my head on one side. "They had three children to care for. Most parents can't do that on one income these days."

"But she's insisting on constantly being Superwoman. She should let him be Superman sometimes. Good for his ego. Good for the kids to see him in a stronger role. Probably good for her to have a rest, too."

I looked at him really directly then. "I bet you did well at vicar school."

He snorted, and then covered his face with a hand. "Theological College," he chuckled from behind his fingers. "I did okay."

"You like people. Knowing what makes them tick."

"Couldn't do the job otherwise," he agreed.

"So what motivation could anyone have for murdering Isobel?"

He shook his head. "Whichever way I think about it – and she's been constantly in my thoughts – I come up blank.

I don't believe for a moment Margaret had anything to do with it. She'll be happy enough to inherit a beachside cottage but she wouldn't kill her sister to get it. All these stories floating around about Isobel blackmailing people don't really ring true, either. I don't know why I was so worried she had it in for me. She was an entirely dependable self-effacing little mouse. Lived an unremarkable life. That cottage has nothing luxurious in it."

"Agree. So do you think it was simply random?"

"What? That Drizzle Bay has a mad killer on the loose? Someone wanting the thrill of knowing what it feels like to take a life?" His face crumpled into an expression of utter distaste. "I certainly hope not. And then we come back to 'why in my church?' because it was a risky place to do it."

"Mishtaken identity?" That was hard to say after the Pinot Gris because I'd had more of it than Paul.

He smiled at me, despite the grim topic. "You're getting tiddly. Or tired. How was your ice-cream?"

I looked down at my plate and found it scraped clean. "Really good, and they were lovely raspberries. How was your sticky toffee pudding?"

"Delicious. Maybe not as good as my mother's, but she sets a high standard."

"Yes, mothers do," I agreed wistfully, thinking of the slightly eccentric curry waiting for me in the old refrigerator at the cottage. Sally Summerfield lives on in all the recipes I absorbed from her while she was alive.

The tables were thinning out. I glanced at my watch;

already ten-thirty. I didn't want the evening to end, but I supposed it had to so I upended my glass and enjoyed the last half inch of the lovely wine.

"Coffee?" Paul asked.

"I won't sleep."

"Merry, he said, "I'm trying to sober you up. You still have to drive out to the Point."

I smiled across at him. "Thank you Paul."

By now I'd had just enough wine to make me indiscreet. With no-one sitting near to us any longer I crooked a finger and beckoned him closer. "I know something from DS Weasel," I murmured.

His eyebrows rose, and he leaned toward me as though indulging a child. "What do you know, Merry?"

"Your church vase wasn't the murder weapon."

"How the... ?"

"He told me because I told him something in return." I was so close to Paul he'd almost gone out of focus.

"What did you tell him?"

I cupped a hand around his ear so I could whisper. "That when I asked Graham who would own Isobel's house now, he said Margaret and Tom Alsop brought the old parents in to update their original will so both daughters inherited it."

I pulled back far enough to see how he'd taken that. Not exactly pleased with their behavior to judge from the crease between his eyebrows and the very direct stare.

"And the vase?" he asked. "I thought they were pretty

sure about that because of the size of her wound and the curve of the vase and so on."

I put my hand back around his ear so I could whisper again, although I was probably drawing more attention to us than being discreet. "No blood or other yucky stuff on it."

Paul suddenly sat up very straight. He grabbed my hand. "We need to go, Merry. We'll forget that coffee if you're okay without it."

"That's fine," I agreed, no doubt sounding puzzled. "Thank you for a nice night." Why had he gone into rabbit-bolting-off mode?

He handed over his credit card and put an arm around me to escort me to the car. Yes, I was somewhat wobbly on the high pink heels after the Pinot Gris, but the crisp night air was a helpful slap in the face. Traffic was still pretty constant because the Burkeville Bar and Grill is ideally situated on the main highway across from the ocean. As each vehicle passed and silence fell for a few seconds, big waves crashed over onto the sand with a rhythmic roar.

"Surf's up," I said. "It'll be hard to sleep at the cottage tonight with the sea making such a noise."

Little did I know...

Paul helped me into the car and closed the door. As soon as he'd fired up the engine he turned the ventilation onto rather cool. It gave me goosebumps on my arms but probably helped bring me to my senses. I reached for the cardi I'd hung over the back of the seat and draped it around my shoulders.

"Okay?" he asked.

I nodded at him.

"Thinking clearly?"

What an odd question.

I nodded again.

I was rather drowsy to be honest, and he didn't try and engage me in further conversation for the fifteen minutes it took to reach the main street of Drizzle Bay.

"Why are we here?" I asked as he pulled up outside St Agatha's. The village was deserted.

"I want to check something," he said. "And I want a witness. You feeling up to it?"

"So that's what the cold air was about?" It made sense now. "There's no blood still in there, I hope?"

"No Merry – all gone. But what you said about the vase? That's got me thinking. There were two matching vases."

I let that sink in for a few seconds. "So where's the other one?" I asked after my tired and tipsy brain caught up.

"Inside," Paul said, opening his door, slamming it, and walking around to my side of the car.

My cardi had got caught around part of the headrest, and we spent a few seconds untangling it so I could put it on. "Whereabouts inside?"

"Up by the pulpit. There are stands for flowers either side of the nave and we generally have a vase on each."

I pushed myself up off the seat and Paul closed the door behind me. I heard the locks click in the deafening silence. Well, deafening apart from the sea.

"Ummm... so there's one vase now?" I asked as he led me past the crime-scene tape and around to the back of St Agatha's. He unlocked the door. "Why do you want to see it?"

He fumbled around the switches inside and snapped one on. Half a dozen small side-lamps glowed golden. It wasn't a lot to see by but Paul was used to his church and seemed to think it was enough. He pushed the door shut again and took my hand, then produced his cell phone and turned on its torch. That was better.

"She always used a little folding table from the vestry to sit the vases on while she arranged the flowers. You probably didn't notice it, having just had such a shock. It was knocked flat anyway." He started leading me forward. "She'd get the flowers looking good, carry each vase to its stand, and then bring the water to the vases because they were far too heavy for her to carry when they were full."

My brain was clearing now. "So that's why there were flowers and pottery shards on the carpet but no water?"

Paul shone the torch further up the aisle, illuminating the single colorful vase of flowers there. "Isobel had the other one sitting beside a pew for the rest of the flowers. It must have got kicked sideways because I remember that WPC picking it up and setting it on its stand out of the way while I was phoning Margaret. I didn't even think about it until you mentioned it, but of course the Police secured the crime scene. I asked if I could rescue the other flowers Isabel had set aside, shoved most of them into that remaining vase, and went to get the water."

"You did quite a good job," I said, inspecting the arrangement. "Tall things at the back, big things in the middle."

He looked at me as though I was his small and silly sister. "I'm a gardener, Merry. I used to help my mother with her herbaceous borders when I was home for school and uni holidays. Delphiniums at the back, daisies and phlox in the center, low-growing aubrietia along the front."

He'd stopped a few steps away from the vase and seemed reluctant to go right up to it. The light from his phone cast unearthly shadows everywhere. Then he cleared his throat and squeezed my hand tighter. "The thing is – maybe whoever hit her used *this* vase and dropped it beside the pew before they left. And the vase she was already arranging flowers in was the one that fell and smashed on the floor?"

"And everyone assumed she'd been hit with that one." My voice sounded pretty shaky.

Paul took a deep breath. "So I thought we'd better come and check this one in case there's any..."

"Blood," I whispered. "Oh Paul." Now it was my turn to squeeze *his* hand.

We approached the vase together. "Better not touch it," I said.

"I've already touched it."

"Even so – in case there are other fingerprints on it?"

Together we leaned toward the back of the big dark vase as Paul illuminated it. There might have been something there. "I can't tell for sure," I said.

"Me either," he agreed. "But maybe there is."

I thought guiltily of the files I hadn't told Bruce Carver about yet. "We need to tell them. Let them have a look in daylight and do their forensic tests. I've got the number in my phone. In my bag. In your car. There's something I need to tell Bruce Carver, too."

Paul was pretty shocked, poor man. Too shocked to ask what else I needed to pass on. Together we returned to the car and I dug out my phone. "Want me to do it?" I asked, finding DS Carver's listing and looking across at Paul. He gave a slight nod.

I hoped I'd be able to leave a message, but luck wasn't on my side.

"Carver," he snapped. Maybe I'd woken him up? "Do you have more information for me, Ms Summerfield?"

I put the phone on speaker. "I do rather." Had he recognized my number? Graham did that all the time.

"Spit it out then."

Euw! "Well," I began. "You mentioned the vase didn't seem to be the murder weapon, but there's another one the same."

I heard him draw a deep breath. "St Agatha's had a pair of vases," I said before he could interrupt. "I've just had dinner with Paul McCreagh, the vicar. I might have had half a glass of wine too much and told him the broken one didn't have any blood on it."

"Might you indeed." His tone was icy.

"And he said there was another one just like it, so we came back and had a look, and we think it needs checking out in case there's any…"

"Blood."

"Um, yes. And there's something else. I meant to phone you earlier this evening but I got caught up feeding Isobel's dogs and getting dressed for dinner."

"Yeeeeessss…" he said in a resigned tone.

"Well, there's a computer out at the Point. In a secret office. I found it quite by chance, and it looks like someone rushed out in a hurry because it's still going. Put to sleep. Not turned off." I swallowed, and glanced across at Paul. His eyes were huge and his jaw had dropped open.

"So I had a quick look," I continued. "There's very strange stuff on it. Files about stealing cars, maybe? And Black Ops. And moving to America. And making soap."

"Soap?" Paul muttered.

"Soap?" Bruce Carver demanded.

"Yes, and I think I know why that's there. It's because Tom Alsop has a secret son with a woman called Elsa Hudson, and she's a soap-maker, and she's currently at a crafting conference out at Horse Heaven in Old Bay Road."

Bruce Carver expelled a long half-whistle of frustration. "I think we'd be more interested in the stolen cars and Black Ops, Ms Summerfield. Where is this computer, please?"

"In a locked office in the locked garage out at the Point. It's quite safe."

Beside me, Paul had recovered somewhat and was trying not to laugh.

"I'll be the judge of that, Ms Summerfield. I'll get a team together and we'll be out there as soon as possible."

"No – I'm not there," I bleated. "Come in the morning. Any time after eight. Hang on." I thrust the phone sideways. "Tell him what time suits you for the vase."

Paul sat there shaking his head at me. "What a dope you are," he said. "Not you, detective," he added hurriedly. "I was talking to Merry. Basically any time's fine. The church is locked. No-one else has the key. I can open up any time at all for you. If you want a look now, no worries, although I don't see the point in disturbing anyone so late at night."

Bruce Carver harrumphed a bit and eventually conceded early in the morning would be fine.

"And you'll need to take my prints," Paul said. "I'd be the last person to handle the vase. I used the other flowers Isabel had brought and put them in the second vase to get them out of the way of your forensics people when they attended to the carpet."

"Understood," Bruce Carver said. "I'll have someone there by eight, and then we'll go on to the Point. I assume Ms Summerfield will be there by then?"

What a cheek! He was practically accusing me of sleeping with Paul and then dashing home at the crack of dawn.

I leaned over and snapped at him, "I'll be there by midnight."

"Then drive safely, Ms Summerfield. And thank you both

for your co-operation." He clicked off before I could say anything else.

"Merry," Paul protested. "Why didn't you tell me? Timing might be really important for those files."

After that comment I certainly wasn't going to let on I'd known about them for the last several days. "I'm sure there's no hurry, Paul. Once I looked at them – only briefly – I was pretty sure it was Tom Alsop's office and not Isobel's. Isobel's dead and Tom's still away cruising, so nothing will be happening."

His brow crinkled. "But why would Tom have an office on Isobel's property?"

"Huh! There's a story there. When I was walking the dogs and stopped to talk to Jim Drizzle about... ummm... whatever it was... he mentioned Tom had got Isobel's family a good deal on that old Mini years ago and then paid to build a garage for it because of the salt spray. Jim had it down as a good deed because the old father drank and they had no money, but once I accidentally found the secret office it all started falling into place."

"Not a good deed?"

"No – he wanted somewhere away from his home and away from his work to keep secret stuff. I'm betting it was a kind of bribe. Let me build this garage but the space down the end is mine. Isobel was definitely using it too, although maybe only recently."

Paul pinched the bridge of his nose. "Are you safe to drive now?"

"Yes, drop me home and I'll collect today's clothes and catch up with Graham if he's still awake. Drizzle Bay Road will be deserted at this time of night."

Paul still looked skeptical. "Lock your car doors while you drive. Text me once you're home."

"Yes, Dad." I rolled my eyes at him.

"And I'll see you in the morning. I'll follow the Police out to the Point."

"They might have arrested you by then." I grinned at him as I slipped my phone back in my bag.

"Not funny," he said, starting the engine. "Apart from anything else, I'd be keen to see this 'secret office'."

———

As I PREDICTED, traffic along Drizzle Bay Road was almost non-existent at this hour of night. I drove my Focus at a nice moderate speed, not wanting to be stopped for going cautiously too slow as though I might have been drinking, or far too fast as though I certainly had. Looking out at the deserted countryside I thought of Paul's advice and clicked the button that locked all the doors. They made quite a noise in the quietly purring car, and I smiled at his protectiveness.

There was a big moon rising out of the sea, and almost no signs of civilization. People were either in bed by now or had their curtains drawn. The vet clinic had a light shining over the front door. The agricultural tanks depot had a surprising blue neon sign with ripples of water flashing on and off. Then there was nothing until Drizzle Farm which had ornate black lanterns on top of its brick gateposts. One lightbulb had blown.

I'd only had the car for a short while and it needed a name. I thought about that as I neared the cottage on the dark road, but I was out of inspiration. Effie for the two Fs in Ford Focus? Aubie for its aubergine paintwork? Something more snappy hopefully, but nothing else came to my tired mind.

The driveway gate was open so I coasted right in and braked close to the garage. I must have rushed out in a fair hurry because I generally latch it, but the dogs always stayed near the cottage, so not a worry.

I could hear them. Barking like fury, but not dashing out to greet me. Maybe they had a mouse bailed up in the vegie patch at the back?

I texted 'Home' to Paul and hopped out. Yes, there was a big sea running. The waves were really pounding. I stood listening for a few seconds, but whatever the dogs had found was more interesting than me. Then, in a sudden rush, a male shape appeared. Not a very big one, but I still had the high pink heels on, and the concrete was cracked and uneven.

"Missy Crombie," the shape yelled, lunging for me. I went down in a heap, and the world turned dark.

14

TAPED AND TERRIFIED

Pinot Gris doesn't give you a headache like this.

Why can't I move my hands?

Why can't I move my feet?

Why can I see all those stars?

Why are those dogs still barking?

I drifted in and out of consciousness for hours. Or maybe I drifted in and out of sleep. Either way, it wasn't good. I ached all over. Couldn't move a muscle. Couldn't say a word because my mouth had something over it. I tried loud moaning, but no-one heard. No surprise there.

I finally worked out I was in Isobel's office. Imprisoned in her chair. Ankles taped together and secured to the central column. Wrists taped together in front of me, and bound against my chest. Pain like I'd never experienced before had spread through all my cramped limbs, and my head was pounding worse than the surf.

With a lot of wriggling I managed to get the toe of one of my shoes onto the floor. Even that seemed like a huge victory, although it achieved nothing.

How had that small man got my five-foot-eight womanly frame into the garage and onto the chair? No surprise he'd been able to open the garage – my keyring would have clattered onto the concrete with me. He'd obviously known all about the office and how to move the shelves. Surely he couldn't have been alone? Thank goodness for my cardi, even though it wasn't super-cozy. And maybe I should be grateful I hadn't been left lying out on the cold ground like a trussed-up turkey. It was hard to feel *very* grateful though.

In the big skylight above me the stars slowly disappeared from the midnight-blue sky as it paled to twilight-blue. Or dawn-blue I suppose. And eventually there was enough light to see the iMac was missing, along with many of the notebooks and folders. I squinted through my disgusting headache, trying to focus on the spines of what was left. Couldn't read a thing.

I was busting for a wee. Thank goodness I'd gone at home before driving back to the cottage but I wasn't going to last much longer. Almost worse was the craving for water. Behind the tape my mouth was dust-dry. There was barely room to move my tongue over my gums for any relief.

I couldn't see my watch of course – not with my wrists secured like that. And there was no computer screen any longer with its helpful time. I managed to push on the concrete floor with my one toe and swivel the chair slowly around. The shelf door was shut and no doubt secured. It had been so much effort to even turn around I didn't bother trying to bump against it to check.

I dropped my head, defeated, then found I was buried in my own hair and slowly raised my face to the sky again. How long before the Police turned up? How long before Paul arrived?

It seemed an age, but finally I heard a noise. It was a lawnmower coughing and roaring and refusing to fire up. Alex must be here! How hadn't I heard the scream of his noisy motor scooter? Had I passed out again? Had he walked from the farm so no-one heard him leaving?

The dogs started up at the lawnmower noise, still sounding some distance away. Well, at least they were alive... I wished I felt alive too.

The garden shed was pretty close to the garage as far as I could recall. With every ounce of my strength I pushed the toe of my shoe against the floor and crashed the chair backward against the edge of the desk, moaning behind the tape at top volume, and grateful my hands weren't taped behind me. I managed it four times before I heard the unmistakable sound of knuckles rapping on the garage window and a man yelling, "Are you in there? Is someone in there?"

A lot of good that was going to do. I moaned and crashed again and finally heard a new noise; something scraping against the wall behind me. Then there was creaking as feet climbed a ladder and a body levered itself onto the roof. A few seconds later Alex stared down at me through the skylight window. His eyes widened with shock. Then he looked across to the road, gave me a thumbs-up signal, and creaked his way down again. The side window of the garage exploded with a huge crash as he hit it with something. Broken glass tinkled down all over the Mini and the floor, accompanied by the slam of car doors and bellows of "Freeze."

He didn't freeze. From the sudden crunch of big boots on shards of glass I concluded he'd vaulted through the window. "Police are coming," he yelled.

I just about wet myself with relief.

"Got the little creep trapped," someone shouted.

I heard banging on the shelves. At the wrong end. Then on the center shelf. Someone else landed on the broken glass and cursed before I heard the instruction, "Freeze," again.

"She's in there," Alex shouted. "Tied up. Let me damn well go!"

"Merry?" That was Paul.

"Round the back, up the ladder," Alex yelled to him. And then, to one of the Police officers; "If my mother hears you've tried to handcuff me, you're dead meat!"

No doubt they'd heard more colorful threats, but I've met Elsa and I'd have been scared. Those eyebrows...

There was more creaking and then I saw Paul peering down at me, twice as shocked as Alex.

"Can we break the glass?" someone shouted.

"No way! We'll cut her to pieces. She's directly under it."

I kept looking up at him. Best sight in the world.

Then I heard the rattle and squeak of the garage door rolling up.

"There's got to be a way in." That was the nasal twang of DS Bruce Carver.

His two officers banged on the shelves and threw things onto the floor to the accompaniment of swearing and grunts of frustration.

"Got it." The latch scraped back and the shelves swung aside.

I'm ashamed to admit I burst into tears. Nothing had ever looked as good as that view of daylight and three men and a boy all staring at me with deep concern.

"We need a knife to cut her free." That was Alex, sounding a lot older than sixteen.

Paul arrived back from the roof the same moment the knife was produced. "My job," he said, reaching for it, kneeling, and carefully severing the tape holding my wrists together. Then he bent lower and freed my ankles. When I tried to stretch my long-confined limbs, excruciating pain flooded through every inch of me. I groaned and sobbed and possibly swore a bit. I didn't need Bruce Carver's overpowering cologne making things worse in the small space.

To my astonishment Paul slid one arm under my knees, the other around my back, and picked me up. "Bathroom?"

"Mmmmmmm...." I laid my head on his shoulder. By contrast, he smelled wonderful.

"Excuse us," Paul said, virtually steamrolling Bruce

Carver out of the way and striding toward the house. "Can someone unlock?"

I realized a bit woozily that if they'd opened the garage they must have found my key-ring.

A uniformed figure dashed past us and I heard the cottage door creak open. Two little white dogs erupted out in a storm of barking. "Poor chaps," Paul said. "Looks like their door's been blocked up all night."

He carried me to the old bathroom and left me in privacy. Oh. My. Goodness. That was good.

Peeling the tape off my face wasn't so good though, although my generous dollops of moisturizer might have greased me up a bit.

I staggered out a few minutes later and limped down the hallway to change into more suitable clothes. To my surprise Alex had the kettle boiling when I returned. "Tea or coffee?" he asked me. "I put the kitchen chairs out in the sun," he added. "And found a couple more. That boss cop stinks."

In possibly the least formal briefing ever, we sat around in the open air on Isobel's old spindle-backed chairs. Alex played waiter, Bruce Carver threw questions, and Paul gave him the evil eye if he got too impatient.

Itsy and Fluffy soon trotted over and sat by my feet, eyes bright and hopeful. "Could you feed these two?" I asked Alex. "Bowls under the table, food in the pantry." He clomped away in the heavy motor cycle boots that were so useful for landing on broken glass.

"The situation has obviously changed," Carver said. "Can

you please confine the dogs to the other side of the house in case they disturb any evidence out here?"

Wheel tracks and so on, I presumed. It didn't seem likely, but I nodded along.

"As you know, we planned to uplift a computer and sundry files to do with car theft, but this is now a serious assault and attempted homicide."

I almost dropped my tea. "No!"

"Days confined without food or water? With the sun beating in through that skylight? The wound on your head untreated?" He turned to one of his men. "Call Doc Hopkins. Tell him he'll soon have an assault victim with a head wound for a looksee. And get Forensics out here. With something to cover that broken window." He sent Alex a glare that was never acknowledged.

"I'll be fine," I protested. "Someone would have found me."

"The back of your head's covered in blood, Merry," Paul murmured. "You're lucky you're not dead already."

I shuddered as I thought of the scene in the aisle of St Agatha's. "Has Isobel's killer tried again? This was quite a small man and he called me Missy Crombie. He wasn't a Kiwi. He can't have been alone or he'd never have managed to move me." I cradled my aching head. "And if he'd already killed Isobel, why call me Missy Crombie?"

"Give it a rest, Merry," Paul said. "Leave it to the experts."

Bruce Carver closed his mouth. It looked like he'd been ready to say the same thing.

"Anyway," I added, feeling gingerly around in my hair, "The computer might be gone but I sent the most interesting files into the Cloud so you can still access those."

Poor DS Weasel's face was a study in contradictions. Relief that all his evidence wasn't lost. Disbelief that I'd do something as outrageous as stealing it. His mouth twitched and his eyes flickered and I saw his Adam's apple bounce several times as he swallowed his pride or his outrage or whatever it was.

I shrugged. "Sorry – they were fascinating. I wanted another look."

"Tampering with Police evidence," he muttered.

Beside me, Paul shook with barely suppressed laughter.

I glared around the circle of men. "I didn't tamper with it in the least. And it wasn't Police evidence until I told you about it." I blew out a long regretful breath. "Shame the emails are gone," I added. "There was one from someone called Hannah Hertzog about retirement facilities in Florida. Sounded like Isobel was planning to move there, but the more I think about the situation the more likely it seems it was Tom Alsop planning to do a runner and using Isobel's name."

"THANK you, Ms Summerfield," DS Carver said with barely restrained fury.

But I was being helpful!

"Would you please get my laptop from the bedroom so he can see the files?" I asked Paul.

When he returned I opened my Dropbox account and

showed Bruce Carver the list of what I'd downloaded. "Do you want me to send them to you?" I offered. "Or maybe to Detective Wick?"

He breathed out quite noisily. "Em dot Wick at police dot govt dot..." he began.

"I'll do it," Alex said. "Say it again."

Bruce Carver produced a card. "Like mine, but with Em dot Wick on the front."

"Got it," Alex said, moving into the shade, ignoring us all, and getting to work.

"The world belongs to the young," I said to Paul. I saw one corner of Alex's mouth kick up but otherwise he ignored us.

"That's probably enough for you now, Ms Summerfield," Bruce Carver said. His face was rather pink and he was gnawing at one of his nasty fingernails. He looked as though he was bursting with regret that he couldn't grill me further. Also that he wanted to get back to his headquarters and check out the files. "I'd like to keep Miss Crombie's garage key for a day or two. I'll definitely have more questions once you've been seen by the doctor and are feeling more lucid."

I was feeling perfectly lucid! I inclined my head in agreement. The sooner they left, the sooner I could make us all some toast.

Paul rose and removed the garage key from my collection. He handed it over. "I'll get Merry to the doctor pronto."

———

"HAVE YOU TWO HAD BREAKFAST YET?" I asked once the deputation had departed.

Heads were shaken.

"Early start," Paul said.

Alex closed the computer. "I was aiming to get the lawns mowed first, but then I heard you banging about."

"And thank heavens for that," I said, sending him a heart-felt smile. "When the mower engine coughed, my pulse rate probably doubled. That was such a good moment. Why did you think it was worth trying the ladder?"

Alex shrugged. "Oskar told me the last time he mowed the lawns he heard a radio going in the garage. He looked through the window in case she'd left the car running, but there was no-one there. Nosy guy. He could see the garage was longer outside than inside so he had a quiet look up top. Just as well, eh?"

I closed my eyes for a second or two. "I'm grateful beyond belief. Okay, breakfast; if neither of you has eaten I can manage toast to keep us all going for a while."

"I'll make it," Paul said.

Alex handed me my laptop. "I'll take the chairs in."

A teenage boy can eat a lot of toast. And marmalade. And peanut butter. And honey. His slice-count probably equaled Paul's and mine combined, and once he was refueled he leaned his elbows on the table, breathed in, breathed out, fiddled with his earring, and finally opened up to us. "Can I tell you something?"

He waited until he was sure he had our attention. "I'm

worried about Mum. She's getting awful headaches. She's really rude to people sometimes because of them." His big eyebrows almost met in the middle as he frowned.

Rude to people, huh? The strange scenes at the Horse Heaven barn swam back into my overtaxed brain. Elsa had snapped something at the goth-girl about Alex being too young for her and called her a 'Peg-people Weirdo' or something else offensive. And she'd turned her back on me pretty swiftly at the table after saying she made soap. I'd offered to buy some and she'd still ignored me. Definitely rude.

"Is she stressed about anything?" Paul asked. "Do you have a dad you can talk to? Any uncles or aunts?"

Alex shook his head. "Just me and her."

I thought of his blurted comment during the phone call asking about mowing the lawns. "You said you were Tom Alsop's son. That you wanted some justice for your mother."

Paul stayed very quiet, giving Alex the chance to answer.

"Yeah... well... he's got a huge house and all those cars, and we live in a crappy old bus. Is that fair? He could make her life a lot better."

The olive green bus with the curtains I'd seen at Horse Heaven... not a great place to grow up. It was a wonder Alex had turned out as well as he had – surprisingly polite and helpful, not covered in obvious tattoos and piercings apart from the black disc in one ear. At home on my laptop, willing to make tea for policemen, and to barbecue bacon and buns for a group of crafters. Jim Drizzle had taken him on for a few days of farm work without turning a hair, and Lord Jim's no fool.

I turned my cup around on the pretty saucer. "Has your mother always had the headaches, or are they new? I can ask Doc Hopkins' advice while he checks out my scalp."

Alex thrust a hand back through his shaggy mane. "Pretty new. She goes mad with them sometimes. Crashes around and... hits things."

"Does she hit *you*?" Paul asked before I could.

"I get out of the way."

Poor kid.

Paul reached for my plate and stacked it on top of his. "Let's get you to the doctor, Merry. Take care of that mess in your hair and see if you need any stitches."

"I don't expect so," I said, shuddering at the thought. "Aren't head wounds supposed to bleed a lot? This seems to have dried off, so it can't be much. You two go and investigate the mower," I added, recalling the splutters of the unresponsive engine. "See if you can get it going. I need a bit of lipstick."

I pushed my chair back and bent down to Itsy and Fluffy. "Do you want a ride? In Paul's car?" I swear they know the words 'ride' and 'car'. They scrambled up, looking eager as always, as Paul and Alex headed out to the garden shed. Mindful I'd been asked to stop the dogs from disturbing any evidence, I put their leads on, looped the ends over the doorknob so they couldn't roam, and went to check out how bad I looked.

Then I remembered the two courier envelopes. How had I forgotten those? Something else for poor Bruce Carver to scowl about...

———

"Are you thinking what I'm thinking?" Paul asked once the mower was happy and we'd driven away from the Point.

"About his mother? That she hits things?" Because of course I was thinking exactly that. I stretched my stiff fingers and then wove them together again in my lap. "Are you wondering if she hit Isobel?"

He grimaced. "She'd have no reason to, but who knows?"

I stayed silent for a while, remembering what had happened at Horse Heaven, and trying to tie it up with Alex's remarks. "I met her at that crafting get-together in Old Bay Road. She's a bit... odd. She looks unkempt compared to the photo on her soap making website. As though she's gone downhill since that was taken."

Paul took his eyes off the road for a couple to seconds to look across at me. "She might be wacky enough to have invented the story about Tom being Alex's father."

We drove on and I turned the situation around and around in my mind. "Alex is tall like Tom," I said. "Dark-haired like Tom used to be. And he's a clever kid. I don't think he'd take Elsa's claims at face value without finding out more. He knows she's unstable. I expect he knows more than he's told us."

Paul nodded slowly, looking grim. "He knew about the Alsops' big house. He's got that scooter to buzz around on. I bet he's been there and had a look. I bet he's been to the car places, too. Probably also wanted a look at Tom."

"Well, wouldn't you, if your mother suddenly announced who your father was? It's just as well the Alsops are away on that cruise."

"It's a shocking position to be put in at his age," Paul said. "Do you think he was telling us she was dangerous and hoping we'd take the weight off his shoulders by passing our suspicions on?"

I shrugged. "So he didn't have to report his own mother? I wouldn't be surprised." I sighed and reached for my phone.

Paul slowed as we reached the village. "They've got the vase. Tell Carver there might be other fingerprints of interest."

He answered straight away – in a tone that sounded like 'not you again' but was actually worded, "Ms Summerfield – how can I help *this* time?"

I felt terrible doing it, but I explained what Alex had told us, and passed on Paul's comment about other possible fingerprints. "She'll be with a group of women at a craft stall outside The Café this morning. They should be setting up fairly soon."

"You're determined to solve this for me, aren't you, Ms Summerfield," he said wearily.

I looked down at the shiny plastic envelopes in the pocket of the car's door. My fingertips were itching. "Just helping," I said. "And I've got two courier deliveries addressed to Tom Alsop we can drop off after the doctor. Shall I open them up and tell you what's in them?" I teased.

I easily pictured his clenched teeth as he turned down my offer.

EPILOGUE

THEY SENT an ambulance for Elsa Hudson even before her fingerprints were identified on the church vase. By then she was incandescent with rage – raving about how she'd got rid of Tom Alsop's wife so he could now marry her and be a proper father to his son. I'm not sure if she ever realized her mistake: short, silver-haired, arranging flowers in the church – but the wrong sister. An aggressive, inoperable brain tumor makes it unlikely.

When the Alsops arrived back from the tropics Tom was arrested for more kinds of car theft than I could even understand. He had fingers in many pies and is now detained in a concrete-floored cell instead of living the high life in the plush Florida retirement facility he no doubt aspired to. Margaret is making the best of things out at the Point after their wildly over-financed mansion in Sandalwood Grove was foreclosed on by the bank. She was out on her ear within hours. No doubt it'll be sold in a mortgagee auction pretty soon. I imagine her jewelry's gone, too. We did a rather uncomfortable swap-over – me moving out of the cottage as she moved in, each of us trying to keep out of the other's way.

Speculation at the Burkeville has been running at fever pitch ever since.

"Isobel knew all about that secret office," I told Lisa as we perched on our bar stools and waited for John to bring our drinks. "Tom had it built for himself for sure, but her household files were there too. He obviously wanted somewhere to keep info that wasn't related to his legitimate car dealerships."

"If any of them *were*," she huffed.

"I guess the Police are going through everything they can find, legal or otherwise. Maybe Isobel got a thrill from letting Tom use her name to protect himself from discovery. Perhaps she felt she was getting one over on Margaret by doing that."

"Seems a bit odd," Lisa muttered.

I leaned closer so I could whisper. "But what if she was secretly in love with him? Maybe she had been for years?"

Lisa blew a raspberry at that idea, then fell silent for a few seconds before looking at me with extreme doubt. "Really?"

"Stranger things have happened."

"Not *much* stranger," she said as John sauntered over with my wine and her vodka and tonic.

"Not much stranger than what?" he asked, setting the glasses down.

"This whole situation between Tom Alsop and the Crombie sisters," I said. "He married Margaret, but he seemed to have some sort of hold over Isobel, too."

John grinned. "There were plenty of stories floating around here but I never saw any evidence."

"Stories? Were there?" I asked, possibly adding a slight eyelash flutter.

"Bar talk. Gossip. All theory and no proof."

"About Tom and Isobel having an affair?" My eyes were probably bugging out.

John's grin faded and he shook his head. "Why is it always all or nothing with women? Not an affair. Business dealings."

"You think she was implicated in the car thefts, too?" Lisa asked.

He reached out for my credit card. "Probably only by letting him use her name as an email contact."

"And her address for courier packages," I inserted. "Two of those arrived while I was house-and-dog sitting out at the Point."

I turned to Lisa. "Speaking of dogs, Isobel's will included a request for Lurline from the animal shelter to find a suitable home for the teddies if by any chance she passed on before they did. I told Lurline Bernie and Aroha Karaka were interested, so don't be surprised if the Bichons turn up at the vet clinic renamed Ahu and Erana."

Lisa laughed. "No more Itsy and Fluffy? Thank heavens for that."

John shook his head as he turned away to serve two newly arrived customers. "Your usuals?" he asked DS Carver and Marion Wick.

"'Fraid so," she agreed, and he set two cups on the espresso machine drip tray.

"Ah, Ms Summerfield," the DS said, catching sight of me. "I have some news about your attacker, the foreign national who mugged you and left you to die."

"*So* offensive being mistaken for an old lady," I snapped. "Honestly, couldn't he tell the difference?"

"He might not have known her age," John said. "You were looking pretty hot that night, so he can't have."

That gave me a small glow of satisfaction. So John had liked my long hair and low neckline? I sent him a smile and got a wink in return.

"Yes, I think we go with that," DS Carver agreed. "He knew we were close on his heels and he needed to make all those files disappear. He says he planned to break in to the garage quietly, thinking midnight would be a safe enough time. It was horribly bad luck you returned right when you did."

"Sounds like you put up quite a fight," Marion Wick said.

I wasn't so sure about that. I can only remember blacking out on the concrete, but who knows what you do when you're semi-conscious? I could have been yelling blue murder and thrashing around like rodeo horse. "You don't think he meant to kill me?"

DS Carver didn't seem keen to answer that. "Obviously

he needed you immobilized so he could ransack the office. I wouldn't like to speculate on more."

"But because I'd uploaded those files to Dropbox you were able to arrest him?"

A slow and rather grudging nod. "He had no idea we had access to them. Wasn't expecting to be tracked down so easily."

"And he spilled the beans on Tom Alsop, hoping for leniency?" I suggested.

"Yes, to a very satisfactory degree. He's a nasty piece of work, and he's being deported to his country of origin because they want him there much more than we want him here. I can't disclose any further details because there's the possibility of a prisoner swap."

"The jails are much nastier there," Marion Wick added, fixing her big eyes on mine for a few seconds, and then letting her gaze wander over to John.

"Poor old Nam Cheng," I said. "I feel kind of bad about that, but only 'kind of'. Who are you going to swap him for?"

I saw John send the DS a look that would have frozen red-hot lava.

"Ah – not at liberty to say, I'm sorry. Negotiations are at a delicate stage, and all that... But it was a disgusting thing to do, leaving you helpless after uplifting anything that might incriminate him."

When I think about that long frightening night, quite a lot of me turns to weepy jelly, so I nodded and tried to switch off, not trusting myself to speak for the moment. I was grateful when a chorus of greetings at the door diverted everyone's attention.

"Just the chap I need," Lord Jim Drizzle boomed as he entered the bar and made his way across to us. "Young Alex said to give you this." He laid a small parcel in a plastic bag in front of Bruce Carver.

"What is it?" the DS asked, giving it a tentative poke.

"The hard drive from Isobel Crombie's computer."

"Or Tom Alsop's computer," I suggested.

"How on earth...?" Marion Wick asked, eyes bigger than ever.

Jim Drizzle beamed. "He's a clever kid, that one. He'll be off to Uni soon, and plans to major in computer science."

"Yes, but how...?" she asked again.

Jim parked his corduroy trousers on a bar stool. "He was riding a quad around the farm and spotted something pale down one of the inclines. Thrown from the road above, and intended for the river, by the looks of it. It was pretty smashed up but it got snagged behind a tree trunk, which stopped it going into the water."

"Her computer? And he took it to bits?" Bruce Carver asked, obviously dismayed.

"Already in bits." Jim's big white eyebrows waggled. "We've got the rest at home, but he says this is all you'll need."

"So that'll have the emails, too?" I asked. "You'll be able to tell if Isobel was ever blackmailing anyone?"

"It's very unlikely she was," Marion Wick said. "I know

there were rumors to that effect but her bank records show no deposits that can't be accounted for."

Huh. So much for what everyone *thought* they knew!

"Something to drink, Jim?" John asked.

"You know my poison," he said, looking up at the row of whisky bottles. "Just a single for the road."

While John scooped ice-cubes into a squat glass Jim cleared his throat and said, "I've offered Alex a base for as long as he wants. I brought that old green bus back to the farm for him. He was all for driving it himself, even though the boy has no Heavy Transport license. He claimed he'd been driving it all year and was a lot safer than his mother."

We all responded with nods and noises of surprise and disapproval.

"So I told him I'd been driving farm trucks and tractors for several of his lifetimes," Jim said. "And that I used to race motorbikes too. That seemed to go down well."

I smiled to myself. Alex might not have found the father he hoped for, but a substitute grandfather was a really good deal. He's offered to type up the first draft of the Drizzle memoir. I await the treat of editing that sometime in the future.

When I'd last seen Bruce Carver I'd plucked up the courage to ask him about the Black Ops files featuring John and Erik. He hemmed and hawed and wouldn't answer properly. I've never heard a man use so many words to say so little. I've concluded they're somehow working for the government as well as running the Burkeville Bar and Grill.

That might explain Marion Wick's exasperated sigh of "Riii-ight... John," when they came out to the cottage to question me.

And Vicar Paul? I have high hopes for him. We'll have to wait and see if he has any in return for me.

THE END

A NOTE FROM KRISTIE

Thank you so much for choosing to read my book! And thank you even more if you write a review. Reviews are what keeps the books ticking over, and the author writing more.

I want to acknowledge here the encouragement of two of my writer friends, Diana Fraser and Shirley Megget. We've been making each other laugh for a very long time and initially planned to write cozy mysteries as a threesome so we could produce books faster for you. But life gets in the way sometimes and we each got tied up with other projects.

I'd also like to thank the members of my local chapter of Romance Writers of New Zealand, and The Ngaio Writers Group. It's great to have people to bounce ideas off.

And most of all, I want to thank my husband, Philip. He's so good at putting up with my eccentric queries and late dinners and computer hassles.

I began my working life as an advertising copywriter at my local radio station in Hawkes Bay, New Zealand. Once I'd saved up enough to go travelling I lived in Italy and London. Then I returned to my capital city of Wellington and worked in TV, radio again, several advertising agencies, and then spent happy years as a retail ad manager. Totally hooked on fabrics, I followed this by going into business with Philip as a curtain installer, working for some of the city's top designers. Quite a turnaround! It was finally time to write fiction. In twenty years I haven't fallen off my ladder once through drifting into romantic dreams, but I've certainly seen some beautiful homes and met wonderful people, some of whom I may just have stolen glimpses of for the books.

To see all my titles, including my cozies, go to my website, krispearson.com. Click on the book covers to see more about each. But be warned – all the contemporary romances I've written under my real name of Kris Pearson are totally different from the Merry Summerfield cozy mysteries. To see only the cozies, go to kristieklewes.com.

Next you can enjoy a free sample of XMAS MARKS THE SPOT. Life should have plenty of fun!

Thank you,

Kristie.

XMAS MARKS THE SPOT – CHAPTER 1

YOU NEVER KNOW what's lurking where you least expect it.

I finished the last bite of my toast and marmalade, slotted the plate into the dishwasher, and grabbed the spare smart-key to my brother's Mercedes because I needed to remove his golf clubs from the trunk. All good so far.

The dogs bounded into the garage with me, barking and sniffing. Goodness – maybe there was a dead rat, because something was definitely whiffy. Dust motes whirled around in the air as I operated the auto-open function and the lid rose. Both spaniels whirled around too, dancing on their hind legs and craning their necks for a better view.

And phew – the *smell* once it was open. I clutched my throat, trying not to throw up. Not a dead rat in the corner of the garage. A dead....? Ummmm? Leg of beef? In the car. All my hair stood on end.

It was laid thoughtfully on a sheet of heavy plastic, so at

least the carpet hadn't got soaked through, but OMG, the stink! On top was a somewhat bloody piece of cardboard with a bold message in black marker pen. BEEFY HALDANE BETTER WATCH OUT.

Who the heck was Beefy Haldane? What did he need to watch out for? Who had put this in Graham's car? And why?

This was no way to start a beautiful summer's day in Drizzle Bay, New Zealand!

Graham is a lawyer, and currently at a legal conference in Melbourne, Australia, which is why I could nick his Merc. I surmised that Beefy Haldane was a client of his who was into something criminal. But how had anyone got an entire leg of beef into a locked car inside a locked garage on a property guarded by two uber-nosy dogs? How had they even carried it? It was enormous.

I hauled on Manny and Dan's collars to stop them trying to eat the evidence, and eventually got them back onto the chains attached to their kennels. They weren't keen to leave a prize like that, and continued to whine and bark and dance about with such fervor I thought they might drag the kennels behind them over the yard. In desperation I tore into the kitchen and brought out duplicate breakfasts. They fell to eating but continued to give me the evil eye for stealing such a treat.

They'd been acting rather strangely for the two days Graham had been away – sniffing around the garage as though they suspected me of locking him in there. Given the walks I'd taken them on, and the generous meals I'd provided, this seemed less than grateful, but now I knew why.

So much for looking forward to having our rather yummy vicar, Paul McCreagh, beside me for an hour and a half while we drove to the airport to collect his sister. She's flying in from England for a Kiwi Christmas. Would the police let me have the car back in time? And how much of that stench could I get rid of, if so?

I'd better explain that I'm Merry Summerfield, a divorced freelance book editor, and I share the family home with Graham after our darling parents left it to us. They died far too young in a nasty car crash. Graham is six years older than my forty-four, and conservative beyond belief – hence his choice of a nice safe car like the Mercedes, and in the same shade of silver grey as everyone seems to choose.

His car is much more suitable than my little aubergine Ford Focus for collecting a passenger who's travelled halfway around the world. She might have heaps of baggage. Her brother, Vicar Paul, certainly expects so, and as his car is currently out of action, I've offered to fill the gap.

Plainly I needed to contact Detective Sergeant Bruce Carver again. He of the severely bitten fingernails and over-applied cologne. Oddly, the latter might be a benefit this time because boy that meat really ponged.

Holding my breath and my cell phone, I approached the car, trying to persuade myself there was no need to be sick on the garage floor. I did my best to take a reasonable photo for him and beat a hasty retreat out into the fresh air again.

DS Carver's card was pinned up on the corkboard in the kitchen – a reminder of poor Isabel Crombie's recent murder in the aisle of Saint Agatha's church. I sent him the photo and then rang.

And wouldn't you know it – he was instantly available instead of roaming the coast interrogating crims and leaving his phone to take messages.

"Ms Summerfield," he said in his nasal Kiwi twang. "I was just thinking about you."

I really hoped he wasn't.

Dismissing any thoughts as to why he possibly could be, I rushed ahead. "Did you get that photo I sent? That's why I'm ringing. I've found a quarter of a cow in Graham's car. It still has its fur on... ummm, hide on. It's black, so maybe it's an Angus."

DS Carver cleared his throat very noisily. "Slow down, slow down, Ms Summerfield. I'm going to record this conversation if that's okay with you?"

I clutched at my long hair with my free hand, imagining him plugging things in or twiddling dials. "Yes, fine." I could hardly turn him down.

"Soooo..." he drawled. "Not to give too much away, because we've been trying to keep this confidential, but Jim Drizzle's farm has been the subject of a couple of rustling raids. If the beast still has its hide on, that could be very helpful."

"Yes, definitely still has its hide on. Could you read that notice in my photo?"

"Loud and clear, Ms Summerfield."

"The thing is; I don't think it's aimed at Graham. Whoever did this laid a sheet of plastic under it to protect the car's carpet. What kind of crook bothers to do that?"

DS Carver cleared his throat again. "Have you touched anything?"

"Euw – you must be joking!"

"I'll take that as a 'no'."

"Yes, that's a no for sure. It stinks. It doesn't seem to be fly-blown, and I guess that's because the Merc's seals are good. Graham's forever going on about them." I gave a nervous laugh. "Actually, it probably *is* fly-blown by now because I left everything open to try and get rid of the smell. Insects will be streaming in there as we speak."

"Yes, yes," he muttered. I could hear his irritation from miles away. "How long since the car was used?"

"Monday. It has to be Monday because Graham flew out to Melbourne early Tuesday. With another lawyer friend who's going to the same conference. They took the friend's car to the airport, so that's why Graham's is still here."

"And explains why you're phoning me instead of him. We'll need to contact him and confirm that."

"Of course you will," I said in a sickly sweet voice. "But don't do it yet for a while because he'll still be asleep. Time difference between Australia and New Zealand, and all that..."

I pictured Graham peacefully snoring in his striped pajamas. I love him heaps, even though I make terrible fun of him sometimes. "He doesn't know about it," I added. "I got on to you straight away because there was no point waking him up and upsetting him. Are you going to send someone to take fingerprints? I could do with some help to lift the darn thing out. It must weigh half a ton."

"Touch nothing!" DS Carver practically barked. "I'll have someone there as soon as I can."

"Good," I agreed. "I need to get it cleaned up because the vicar and I will be collecting his sister and her luggage in it this evening. She's flying in from England."

"Is she indeed?" DS Carver said in a voice dripping with suspicion. I don't know why, because right now Heather McCreagh was probably still high over the Pacific Ocean, and she would possibly have been high over Heathrow when the beef was ladled into Graham's car.

"She's landing in Auckland about now, being collected by an old school friend for lunch, and arriving in Wellington around five tonight."

There – that was all I knew. "I'm going to duck down to the shops and buy some air freshener because we don't seem to have any," I added. "Only be gone five minutes."

I disconnected while he was still hemming and hawing. There'd be plenty of time later to answer anything else, and for sure there'd be plenty 'else' if I knew him.

I went outside and peered into the garage again. Some buzzy flies had already arrived, attracted no doubt by the smell of very ripe meat in the hot summer air. Oh well, too late now. I left the car open but closed the garage door. Then

I pulled my exuberant hair up into a ponytail, swiped a bit of lippy on, and hid my un-made-up eyes behind my biggest, darkest sunglasses, reminding myself not to take them off while I shopped.

I locked the back door to the house and hopped into my Ford Focus. Within minutes I was in Drizzle Bay village. At nine-thirty on a weekday morning the shops were quiet, Christmas lights along their veranda edges twinkling merrily but more or less invisibly in the bright sun.

As I trotted past the cafe, chubby cheerful Iona Coppington dragged some lightweight chairs out to put beside the tables she sets up each morning and pulls in again late every afternoon. "Chocolate cupcakes with caramel fudge frosting," she bellowed as I hurried by.

"Put one in a bag for me. Back in a mo," I responded, knowing I shouldn't or I'd end up the same size as her. The woman could cook, that's for sure, but I'd have to give up my toast and marmalade breakfast habit and eat something sawdusty and low-cal if I was going to scoff many more of her glorious treats. Sighhhh...

I wondered what sort of lingering fragrance Heather McCreagh would prefer. I dithered between Eastern Rose and French Begonia. I might not know much about gardening, but I'm pretty sure begonias have no scent in the real world.

———

I DECIDED NOT to alert Graham. Why wreck his day? DS Carver would be sure to do that perfectly efficiently. Clutching the Eastern Rose air freshener, I collected and paid for my cupcake and zipped home again.

Should I tell you that Drizzle Bay is named after Jim Drizzle's family farm, and not the weather? It's on the coast of New Zealand's North Island. The southern part of the North Island, to be precise. There are a couple of other small settlements nearby – Burkeville on the highway north, and Totara Flat – inland and very rural. Not a lot happens around here, and that's the way we like it.

I made sure the gate was locked behind me and headed inside. Off came the sunglasses, on went the eye make-up, and I fluffed around with my hair for a while in case there were any particularly attractive and available fingerprint men.

No, but at least they turned up promptly. After taking assorted photos they dragged the huge piece of cow from the car by lifting the corners of the plastic sheeting so nothing gross escaped onto Graham's precious carpet. Then they removed the carpet and the lining! I hadn't expected that, but maybe there'd be some sort of evidence on it. Just as well Graham wasn't there to see his precious baby being dismantled. This was followed by closing the garage doors so they could spray their special blood-finding chemical around. It's called luminol – I remembered that from editing a series of lurid crime thrillers for a woman called Bree Child (and I didn't think that was a clever pen-name in the least.) No blood showed up on the floor, which was probably a relief.

During the whole time the spaniels whined, howled, and tugged at the ends of their chains by the far fence. I've no idea how they didn't break their necks.

I tied my hair back in a pony-tail after they'd gone, and weeded the pots either side of the garage door – really the only gardening I bother with. DS Carver arrived later. He had Detective Marion Wick with him again – she of the huge, attractive eyes and unfairly slim body.

Why do some people have all the luck? She could probably eat Iona's cupcakes every day and never put on an ounce. (Of course she might go running, too, and spend a heap of time at the gym.)

"Coffee?" I asked. They predictably turned it down so I led them through to the big front sitting room with its view out over the sea. We went around and around in circles with the questions because I really couldn't tell them much more than what I'd reported on the phone, and I'd already handed on Graham's cell phone number so they could ring him.

"Who's this Beefy Haldane?" I asked when DS Carver finally stopped to draw breath.

"Ah," he said unhelpfully.

"Something to do with the cattle rustling?" (Or possibly sheep rustling for all I knew.)

"Connected. Connected," he conceded while Detective Wick opened her eyes even wider.

"Connected to Graham as well?" I pressed.

"It's too early to know," DS Carver stated, resting his elbows on his knees and leaning further toward me. I edged away to avoid the cologne, which even toward the end of the morning was still super strong.

Marion Wick smelled fantastic by comparison. Once again I imagined her cuddled up to John Bonnington from the Burkeville Bar and Café with him sniffing her neck and dropping kisses down the front of her shirt. I had no actual evidence of such a liaison, but plenty of suspicions.

"Well, he's got to be connected somehow, doesn't he?" I suggested. "Otherwise, why choose Graham's car? And how did anyone unlock the garage, unlock the car, avoid making the dogs suspicious, and then lock everything up again? In fact it might have been two people because that meat weighed a ton."

DS Carver chewed the inside of his cheek for a few seconds. "We have a theory... and *only* a theory at this time... that the car may have been tampered with in the parking lot at his place of work."

Huh! Not so stupid after all.

"But keep that to yourself please, Ms Summerfield. Currently we have no reason to believe your brother is involved in anything illegal."

I'm sure my eyes shot so wide open they became at least as large as Marion Wick's. "I certainly hope not!" I said in my best huffy tone. "He's a lawyer. He doesn't need extra money, and he's boringly trustworthy." I tossed my head and my pony-tail whacked the back of my neck. "For what it's worth,

I like your parking lot theory. I would have heard the dogs if it had been done here."

"You haven't been away on any of your pet-minding assignments?" Detective Wick asked.

"This week I'm pet-minding right here at home," I snapped, adding a sniff to emphasize that fact.

There didn't seem to be much more to say on either side, so they were gone well before lunchtime. I slipped into the garage, sprayed another dose of Eastern Rose inside the car, and retired, coughing, to let the spaniels off their chains now there'd be no-one else to chase.

———

"Hi, Paul," I said as the vicar pulled his front door closed later that afternoon and the shiny brass knocker bounced with a bang on the equally shiny striker plate fixed to the glossy red enamel paint. He's painted the church railings, too, and old Peggy Leghorn's back porch. Jasper Hornbeam is the village's 'official' handyman, but Paul McCreagh likes doing practical jobs too, as long as he can fly under the radar. They sometimes team up, and I think they both enjoy the DIY and the company.

I looked up at the sky. "Our fine day seems to be clouding over. It'll be a pity if Heather's first sight of Drizzle Bay is through actual drizzle."

Paul's far too tempting for a man of God. There's at least six feet of him, topped by a thatch of short wavy dark hair which matches his mobile eyebrows and dark brown eyes.

He laughed at my 'drizzle' comment. He's too kind not to. "Do I look okay?" he asked.

Any other man would be fishing for compliments, but I'm sure he simply wanted assurance that his sister would approve of his appearance. Dark grey trousers, sage green shirt, shiny black shoes. Totally respectable, and not a hint of churchiness about him. Interesting.

"Very impressive," I assured him. "You look exactly right for Graham's posh car. Hop in, because I have a ridiculous story to tell you."

He raised one of the aforementioned eyebrows before pulling the passenger door open and settling into the leather-upholstered seat. He sniffed. "Does your brother like roses?"

I grinned as I navigated out into the road. It's a beautiful car to drive but I was conscious of its size, not to mention its price tag. "That's part of the ridiculous story. I went out to the garage early this morning to remove Graham's golf clubs so there'd be plenty of room for Heather's luggage and instead I found a quarter of a cow and a threatening notice."

I glanced over briefly to see how he'd taken that.

"Good grief woman, you attract trouble," he said in a surprisingly mild tone. "I'm guessing the threatening notice wasn't meant for you, though? Why would anyone have it in for Graham?"

"It wasn't meant for Graham, either. Have you come across anyone called Beefy Haldane?"

I saw him swallow. "Dammit," he said. "He's not a good person to know, Merry. A real loner. A wild man. And I mean that in the sense of a man who lives miles away from civilization and seems to live only by his own rules."

The lights on the railway crossing ahead of us started to flash, and as I drew nearer the frantic 'ding-ding-ding' of the warning signal became audible. Once I'd brought the big quiet car to a halt I turned to Paul and said, "It wasn't from this Beefy person to Graham. It was telling Beefy to watch out, but someone had broken into Graham's car and left it there."

I found the photo on my phone and passed it over to him while we were stopped. "Graham's in Melbourne. That's why I could pinch his car when yours packed up. I tried ringing him, but I timed it really badly because he was on the point of giving a speech. I'd already called the cops and it's in their hands now." I looked at Paul more closely. "So how do you know Beefy Haldane? A loner and a wild man? He doesn't sound like a church-goer."

Paul remained silent for a few seconds and then said with obvious reluctance, "There was an incident out at my Totara Flat church a few weeks ago. He smashed the lock with the big stone we use as a door-stop. There's no money kept there. The old chap who gives me a hand with the lawns called me and said there was a madman inside."

I drew a sharp breath at that. "And I suppose you tore off on your own to investigate?"

He jerked a shoulder. "I expected a teenager with a bad attitude. Instead I found a man who looked more like a bear – all hair and incoherent growls. My church stank of cannabis, and he'd located the communion wine, too. All gone – not that there was much of it. He was waving a rifle around and taking pot-shots at the rafters."

For the second time that day my gorge rose and I thought I might be sick. "Paul!" I exclaimed. "He could have killed you."

"Yes," he agreed, and the corners of his mouth pulled up in the faintest of grins. "But I do have heavenly protection, you know."

"Does that work with drunken madmen?"

He nodded very slowly. "There are some benefits to having been a chaplain in Afghanistan, Merry. We had a long talk about guns."

I know my eyebrows rose. I almost choked, huffing in a surprised breath and having to cough a couple of times.

"He was very keen to get his hands on a military style assault rifle now they've changed the gun laws," Paul continued. "Of course I have no idea how to get one," – he rolled his eyes at me – "but I managed to keep him talking until he calmed down, came to his senses somewhat, and staggered out. He took off across the open countryside on the muddiest motorbike you ever saw."

"Thank heavens for that."

Paul rubbed a hand across his mouth. "There's one other thing."

If ever I'd seen a man who didn't want to talk about something, here he was.

He cleared his throat, stayed silent for a while, and finally said, "You remember I told you about Roddy – the army chap who followed me to New Zealand, uninvited?"

At that moment the freight train reached the level crossing and roared across, making further conversation impossible until it had rattled by. Even the superior sound-proofing of the Merc wasn't a match for a diesel electric engine at full speed and its following collection of rushing, clanking flat-beds with multi-colored shipping containers and piles of de-barked logs from the forests further north. Paul and I looked at each other with apologetic shrugs, unable to continue until we could hear each other again.

It gave me plenty of time to remember Roddy. The poor man's surname was Whitebottom. I've heard of Winterbot-toms, which are pretty bad, and Ramsbottoms which aren't much better, but Roddy's name took the cake. He'd come to Paul for counseling in Afghanistan when his promiscuous behavior got him into trouble, read more into Paul's concern than religious care, and turned into a real nuisance. Turned up in Drizzle Bay, too, and had to be gently but firmly turned away.

Finally the signal gave up its frantic dinging and the lights stopped flashing.

"We had to mend a few holes in the roof," Paul said.

"Good thing it was corrugated metal and not hundred-year-old slates or Marseilles tiles. We'd have had a job matching those."

I accelerated smoothly away and onto the main highway. The rear view mirror told me there were plenty more vehicles following us. It's amazing how traffic builds up, even in such a small place. "So he took off on a motorbike and you were okay?" I was much more interested in Paul's safety than the state of the church roof.

"I called the police of course, but as he wasn't on a public road and seemed to be heading for the hills, I think they concluded he'd be safely out of everyone's way for a while."

"And was he – um – 'known to the police' as they say?"

Paul nodded. "Known many times over. As a nuisance rather than a criminal, but the gun got them rattled. I don't think they'd tied him to firearms before."

I wasn't letting him get away with raising a topic like troublemaker Roddy and then dropping it. "Yes, so what about Roddy?"

Paul wiped a hand across his mouth again, still holding the words in, but eventually said, "It turned out Beefy Haldane was who Roddy went bush with."

"Well, they'll make a great pair," I said unkindly. "A hairy bear and your delicate friend."

"*Not* my friend," Paul grated. "He's a good shot, though. And a mischief maker. I don't imagine they're up to any good together."

I gnawed on my bottom lip. "There was nothing about the church break-in in any of the news feeds."

"No. They told me they thought he was part of something bigger and they wanted to stay quiet about it for a while."

I immediately thought of the possible rustling on Jim Drizzle's farm. Lord Drizzle, to be correct. As the last surviving member of a noble old English family he's inherited the title, but seems a lot happier being a New Zealand farmer than an English lord. He does pop over to England periodically though and do a bit of voting in the House of Lords – no doubt on matters that influence the sale and importation of the beef and lamb he produces.

I looked sideways and caught Paul's eye. "Well, I'm swearing you to silence on this, but I dug a little nugget out of DS Carver this morning. They're investigating some local rustling. Part of a cow left in Graham's car... beef of course... and a warning message for Beefy Haldane. Possible, you reckon?"

His eyes narrowed. "Rustling? Good grief – are we in the Wild West?" He reached up and adjusted his sun visor against the bright overcast sky. "I wouldn't put it past them though."

We were coming up to a notorious bend where the Police often waited for speedsters. Sure enough they were there again, right as the lime green and black 'boy-racer' car that had been following me too closely chose to overtake with a great roar and a cloud of stinky smoke. I hope they got a good shot of its registration plate.

"Pack of fools," I muttered.

Paul nodded, and then surprised me by grinning. "We were all young once."

"I was never *that* young," I protested.

"I'm sure you were a very proper young lady," he said, smile undimmed.

I turned the ventilation up a notch in the hope it would hurry the departure of the cloying rosy fragrance and the new whiff of stinky smoke. And possibly cool down any extra pink in my cheeks. "I would have been trying to evade the clutches of Duncan Skeene at that age. And not entirely succeeding."

"Your barely lamented ex?" His gaze sharpened and I wondered, not for the first time, if Paul was interested in me as more than a friend. I also wondered if I would ever make a suitable wife for a vicar. They might not be allowed to marry anyone who's been divorced – another thing I needed to Google, although Prince Harry now has his Meghan...

And I'm probably getting way ahead of myself here.

See more about the Merry Summerfield Cozy Mysteries on kristieklewes.com

Printed in Great Britain
by Amazon